D1343146

SEESAW

Carmel Doohan was born in Birmingham. She studied Fine Art in Nottingham and has lived in Bristol, London and Glasgow. She has a PhD from the University of Glasgow and teaches creative nonfiction at Bishopsgate Institute. She lives in a village on the edge of the Peak District with her partner and young daughter.

'In its intimate and dazzling constellation of anecdote and memory, *Seesaw*'s form seems to be exquisitely composed by the very alliances of correspondence, analogy and sympathetic magic that its narrator dare not believe in . . . I know that this novel, and its searching, unafraid narrator, will stay with me for a long time.' – Daisy Lafarge

SEESAW

Carmel Doohan

First published in 2021
by CB editions
146 Percy Road London W12 9QL
www.cbeditions.com

Printed in England by Blissetts, London TW8 9EX

ISBN 978–1–909585–42–3

For Pete
– who makes the impossible possible

I

The pile is tailed, legged and eyeless; a mischief of rats crowding at their mother's teated flank. You can see the blue meat inside them, their organs like small dirty patches, their skin so translucent that you can see the milk passing through and turning their stomachs white.

The seesaw is red and at either end there is a wooden doll shaped like an old-fashioned clothes peg. The figures have blue bodies, yellow wool for hair and blank, pink faces. When you pull the toy by its string, it trundles along, the dolls moving up and down and up and down.

On Facebook someone has posted a clip of old film that has been digitised. The scratched frames show a factory work-shop where two women in skirts and blouses are wrapping wooden spheres with newspaper. They spread wallpaper paste on with their hands and lay paper strips onto the spheres, occasionally looking expressionlessly into the camera. In the next scene, they are adding strips of bur-gundy leather and putting the dark red balls on a wooden rack to dry. Once there, the globes oscillate gently.

Now there are three women at a workbench. The one in the pink cardigan with pearlescent buttons sponges paste

1

onto strips of coloured paper and lays them over one of the burgundy balls. In a close-up, it becomes clear that the woman beside her is smoothing on a section of West Africa, the deep yellow tones of its landmass complementing her mustard polo neck and gold, clip-on earrings. The dark-haired woman next to her has a palette of ochre, mauve, myrtle and jade, and is using a fine paintbrush to touch up the seams in the Levant. In the final scene, a man places each globe onto a wire stand and uses a spray gun to add a layer of laminate shine.

T om and I are in the van driving from Glasgow to Birmingham to visit my parents. The rain is fierce. As lorries pass us, spray covers the windscreen and we are plunged under water. The screen clears to find us dry but gasping, Tom gripping the wheel. The wipers have a noisy scrape as they smear the screen then clear it, the reality outside shifting between filmic bokeh and HD wet motorway. My hand is on his leg, or his hand, shifting as he shifts gears. Cocooned in the car, he tells me things; one time he told me that he wanted to have a son and teach him something real. Or a daughter. Teach them things that are useful.

The van only picks up the radio in sporadic bursts. Tom twists the dial and it tells us that we are building a new 25-million-pound prison in Jamaica. David Cameron, during a visit to the island, is asked about reparations. He replies: *This is about the future relationship and about what we should be doing together economically in terms of trade and investment.* He explains how the prison's construction is to be paid for out of the foreign aid budget and will house around 300 Jamaicans who are currently serving sentences in the UK. *That is what this visit is about,* Cameron says. *It's about talking sensibly about the future.*

It's at times like these this, despite the fact that he clearly does not come from Stoke-on-Trent, that David Cameron reminds me of my father. Both appear to suffer from a similar confusion about the way that the past connects to the present, both men imbuing the sensible with the same fixed meaning.

When we first got together, Tom asked me why I didn't drive. He loved being behind the wheel and had learnt the moment he turned seventeen. I told him it just wasn't my thing.

'Change was a weird thing for me when I was growing up. It was like something that wasn't allowed to happen.'

Tom's eyes were on the road. 'Isn't change the only certain thing?'

'I don't know.' Cows in a field and beyond them, a row of trees. 'That's what they say, but I think you have to know how to let it in. Also, if you make fake changes fast enough, you can avoid real ones.'

'What are fake changes?'

'I don't know. They look like changes, but aren't.'

'How do you know the difference?'

I shrugged. 'Hindsight.'

What kinds of things would he teach our kids? What would he consider useful? I try to teach myself useful things as I roam the warrens of Wikipedia. Windscreen glass, for instance, is called sandwich glass. It is made from two layers of glass with a thin layer of vinyl sandwiched in between them for strength. This construction allows the glass to remain bonded even when shattered. In the event of breaking, all the bits are held in place by the interlayer, the polyvinyl butyral. Polyvinyl butyral, ethylene-vinyl acetate. It's good to have the names for things, to know what's materially possible.

When I get up on Sunday morning, Mum is at the dining-room table wearing headphones, a *Go Portuguese* textbook open next to her.

'*Pode dizer-me o caminho mais rápido para a praia?*'

This is new. My parents retired last year and they went on holiday to the Algarve to celebrate.

'*Eu gostaria de ir nadar.*'

I am standing in the doorway, the too-bright sunlight flooding in through the bay window, making the table's mahogany veneer shine.

'*Gostaria de vir comigo?*'

Mum turns and sees me. I used to think we could feel it when another person was looking at us because of our reptile brain. The bit in charge of feeding, fighting, fleeing and fucking; the survival instinct part that lets us know when a predator is watching. Mum widens her eyes and holds up a hand. She mimes listening while she listens, then presses stop.

'I didn't know you were there!' she shouts, then takes off the headphones and repeats herself in her normal voice.

'You're sounding good,' I tell her. She puts her notebook back inside the textbook to save the page.

'Oh, it's nonsense. All this to ask someone how to get to the beach and not be able to understand their answer.'

I've been reading about the brain. About how the old idea of a three-part structure – the primal reptilian part, the emotional mammalian part and the newer, smarter neo-cortex – is no longer considered correct. The idea, now, is that we can understand our brains by noticing our response if we take a sip of coffee when we are expecting tea. The argument is that our brains are *predictive engines*, always trying to guess what's coming next. We think we are seeing, but what we are actually doing is comparing: all incoming signals are held up against a vision that we have already made, a picture based on past experience.

Seeing Mum at the table doing her Portuguese makes me realise that I've never really seen her doing something like that before, something just for herself. She and Dad married young, found jobs, bought their house and had us. The main thing they seemed to want from us growing up was that we were good. To be good and to not make a fuss. I can remember, when I was around eight, asking Mum what being good *meant* – but she said not to ask such daft questions. When we went to mass on Sundays we wore something nice and Dad reminded us to thank God for making us so lucky.

On Saturday afternoon, I leave Tom watching the football with Dad while Mum and I go to the shops. I'm in a cubicle, trying on a shirt, when I get a call. I pick up my phone. The shirt is already making me sweat. It's an unknown number.

'Hello?'

'Hello, it's Kirsty here. I hear that you've been involved in a car accident that wasn't your fault. Is that right?'

I hang up and stare at myself in the garishly lit mirror. The loud pop remix pumping through the changing room seems to be speeding up. I put my own top back on and give the hangers of untried clothes back.

I find Mum by a display table of leggings. A woman beside the accessories rack is holding down a crying toddler, trying to strap him into his buggy. It's only ten o'clock but Primark is already busy.

We walk through the rows of clothes, stepping over things that have slipped onto the floor.

'Look at that! And only £3.99.'

Mum puts the pink top in her basket and we comb through the hangers, sometimes pulling something out and holding it up in front of ourselves. I pick up a short dress with a polka-dot print.

'That'd look good on you. You should get it.'

Again, this is new. We walk around a bit more and then make our way to the tills. As Mum hands over her card to pay for my dress, I realise she has put the pink top back.

These days, since she retired, Mum and I can almost talk of the past. Her waters broke early and without warning during the Falklands War. Identical twins, they told her; *The Sun* heralded our birth with the headline *GOTCHA*. Sometimes she says, If we did it again, I would do so many things differently. Usually I say that you can only know what you know when you know it, or that you did your best with the information you had.

Once I said: 'But, even now, with all we now know, *how* would we do it differently?'

Mum said: 'I'd make more time. More space. I'd make myself see.'

Time, space, mass and force. Perhaps, if we spin everything around fast enough in a Large Hadron Collider, we'll find out how it started.

I try to explain some things to Tom on the drive back home. It's hard. Sometimes it seems like he doesn't understand at all how our insides can be shaped and fixed by silent, invisible moments. He says I'm being vague; I try again:

'It's like it's only as you get older that you realise how much your insides, your *actual organs*, have been formed by all these tiny moments.'

'You're doing what your dad does.'

He steps so blithely into such dangerous territory. 'Meaning?'

'You're using *you* instead of *I*.'

It's true; when my dad describes things and how he feels about them, he uses the second-person pronoun in its plural form. Telling a story of someone who has upset him, he says, You feel awful, you feel like that's a real piss-take. It is a royal *you*. I don't know if it's an Irish thing, but it's a conversational stance that takes agreement and complicity for granted.

'Well, I do mean you plural,' I say. 'I mean *you* like *we*, like *we humans*. I mean that this is something that happens to all of us. It's only because you – singular – *like* the shapes that got made inside you that you don't notice it.'

He watches the road as he thinks. It is no longer raining. 'But what you're saying just sounds so passive. Don't we get to make ourselves?'

T om's first gift to me was on his return from a work trip to Sri Lanka. It was a pink flower stuck to a piece of paper and pressed between the pages of a guidebook. Next to it was written the word *Shiva*.

For so long it had not been able to happen, and then it did. Sitting on my bed, he had handed me written confirmation of the first shibboleth, then an hour later, sweaty and hot-skinned beside me, he had whispered the second:

'You feel amazing.'

'Yeah? What do I feel like?'

His fingers stilled. 'You feel like – like a conker.'

I moved myself towards him, pushing his fingers further inside me.

'What does Shiva mean?' I'd asked him. I knew what Shiva meant.

'It's the god of destruction.'

'Why is the god of destruction part of my present?'

We were sitting on the bed. He told me that he had asked someone in a temple why there were so many shrines to the god of destruction. They had told him that there had to be destruction to make way for creation.

'And why the flower?'

'It was growing on a beach we visited. It was the beach where the Tamils were massacred at the end of the civil war. It looked just like an ordinary beach, but then behind the sand dunes there was this trail of stuff. All these brightly coloured things. Clothes and bags and everything thrown on the ground.'

Tom only wore second-hand clothes, hand-me-down T-shirts and jumpers. He had an old stitch picker from his mother's sewing kit that he used to remove any logos and extraneous details from whatever he found in charity shops. For a bag he used an old bike pannier and his sunglasses had come free with a pack of razor refills. They had Gillette stamped along one of the arms.

'A prosthetic leg?'

'Yeah.' He lay back on the bed. 'It was on the sand with all the other stuff, pots and pans and flung-open suitcases. There was an official noticeboard with all this government information about the military victory and the end of the civil war, but the clothes hadn't even been cleared away.'

I lay back beside him, and after a while I asked how the word connected to the flower.

'I don't know – I thought you might.'

Later, I looked up the events on Mullaitivu beach. A trail of paraphernalia leading to a plaque telling you someone else's version of events. Two clicks and all the information, with pictures, is mine. Tens of thousands of Tamils were killed and the argument over the name for the anniversary of the massacre has gone on for years: Genocide Day, Commemoration Day, Celebration Day, Remembrance Day, Victory Day.

These unfamiliar facts have nowhere to rest but meta-phor. What right have I to these fragments? Yet I add them to my swirling pile of grist. A twisted cardigan, a smashed TV set and a plastic shoe in the sand. Other people's stories and other people's pain: I pull them in and let them cluster, half understood, unacted-upon, yet now somehow mine.

A few days later, I'm cycling to work when my phone rings. I stop and shift onto the pavement. Another unknown number.

'Hello?'

'Are you driving?'

'What? Who is this?' My voice sounds loud and shrill on the empty street.

'Are you driving? I can't talk to you if you're driving.'

'I'm not driving. Why would I be driving? Who is this?' I can feel a panic rising in my chest. 'Who is this? I don't know who this is.'

'I'm calling because our records show that you have had an accident.'

The panic fades. 'What the fuck? This is some insur-ance company? Where are you getting my number from?'

'Our records show . . .'

I hang up and cycle on.

As I've said before, I don't drive. When people ask why not, I say things like, Have you seen me reading a map?! Have you seen how bad I am at maths?! This obviously doesn't explain anything, but the latent sexism signals the presence of a joke and steers the questioner elsewhere.

On my route to work, an old iron footbridge crosses the river. On it, someone had sprayed the words *Play Your Part* in bright pink. About a fortnight later, above it in thick permanent marker, someone else added *Feel Free Not To.* As I pass beneath it, I think of the house beside the harbour that I lived in when I was twenty-two, twenty-three. How one night, one of my flatmates called us over to the window to see a car roll into the water. By the time we'd run outside, the car had disappeared. We stood on the cobbles, asking each other what we should do.

'What if someone is trapped in there?'

'Can you see any movement?'

'We should jump in.'

James took off his jumper, Rob took off his shoes and I thought about how cold the water looked. We asked each other the same questions again:

'What if there's someone trapped inside?'

'There'd be movement, wouldn't there be movement?'

'Can you see anything?'

I think James called 999 in the end. The operator asked us if we saw anyone in the car. He told us someone would look into it, but not to worry; it was probably just joy riders dumping a stolen vehicle. That this kind of thing happens all the time. Eventually, we stopped staring at one another and down into the black water and went back inside. Every time I pass this bridge, I feel that moment. Looking into the water and at each other, all of us now knowing what we now know.

I n Glasgow we are staying with our friend Dan until we can find a place to rent ourselves. He has a six-year-old son, Max, who stays with him on weekends and on Wednesday nights. He can be very articulate, but mostly he just moves from bedroom, to hall, to kitchen, holding two of his action figures and making death noises: Pow, pquew, yah, peuw. Aaag, uuurgh, uh. Pquew, pyah!

I look at pictures of cagoules and read about the different levels of dryness: shower-proof, water-resistant, water-proof. I watch a video of Robert Gore's son restaging the moment his dad invented Gore-Tex: Bob is heating yellow plastic rods – polytetrafluoroethylene – in a special oven that looks like a toaster. Frustrated, he grabs one of the hot rods, yanks it sharply and something gives. The rod stretches into a sudden excess, reams of flaxen ribbon cascading onto the floor.

The coat I chose is sequoia red. Breathable, with an adjustable hood.

Dad is very worried about the Rangers pub next door.

'I've emailed you the fixture list,' he tells me on the phone. 'They're already at the top of the division. They'll be playing Celtic again soon.'

Dan's flat is a few streets down from the Ibrox Stadium, but football means nothing to me. Tom is Scottish, so I ask him about it.

'I guess we could afford not to be involved. The whole sectarian thing and the football thing too. It was more important in some places than others.'

Dad keeps worrying about it, though. Worrying about

what he'll do if he comes up to visit and he hears one of those men singing one of their songs at him.

We are in the lounge. Dan is doing his tax returns and Tom is playing chess on his phone. We can hear Max making his soldier noises in the hall. He only plays WWII with his figures – more recent wars don't have the clarity of roles that he requires.

'Did you see that picture?' Dan asks. 'Someone put it on Facebook – the fight in the Ukrainian parliament and the golden section?'

Max runs in. 'Dad, Dad.'

'What?'

'Whose side were we on again in the Second World War?'

'The Allies, Max. The Allies.'

He runs back out. Dan finds the picture and I go over to the table. A group of politicians; one man is throwing a punch, but someone has pulled a jacket over his head. Another man is crouching, but someone else's hands are covering his eyes. The intense light makes the blues and greys of suits glow oily against a dark background of polished wood. The girl who posted it has overlaid a spiral and a series of rectangles onto the photograph.

'Oh, that's great.'

'It was taken by the court photographer.'

'Such good instincts. What were they fighting about?'

'It doesn't say.'

Fibonacci's spiral and the divine proportions of the golden ratio. The blinded men converge and align on the golden rectangle's horizontal dividing line and at the centre of the spiral, exactly where the focal point would be in a Renaissance painting. I went to a lecture on it before I dropped out of art college. All elements cohering in the most aesthetically pleasing arrangement.

S itting on the bed in Dan's spare room, surrounded by the boxes and binbags that contain everything we own, Tom and I scroll through Right Move. Each fish-eye lens photo of other people's badly lit interiors holds a flickering of our new life. Each floor plan is a not-to-scale *tabula rasa*: Tom naked at that sink in the sunlight, his back warm as I stand behind him; having sex on that sofa; waking up in that bed. Pictures, pictures, pictures until our eyes ache.

The radio is on and identical male voices are urging us to be sensible. Through the kitchen window I watch the elderly man who lives in the block opposite stand in the sliver of grass between his window and the car park. His wife is often out there too, a brightly coloured hijab and a red plastic watering can. There is a line of green shoots at the base of the building and the man is inspecting the row of broad beans that climb up the wall. Dan says he has spoken to him once but his English wasn't good. The only moment of communication they had was via the word *potato*.

Max appears in the doorway.
'Where's my dad?'
'Didn't he just go out to move his car?'
'He's been gone ages.'

I've peeled a butternut squash to grate in the food processor. 'I'm going to buzz the machine now.'

Max shouts over the noise. 'He's been gone ages.'

I shout back that he'll be here in a minute, then switch the mixer off and empty the grated squash into a bowl. I smile at him.

'He'll be back in a minute, I promise. Do you like squash?'

He tips his head to one side. 'I only like Ribena. Or Irn-Bru.'

He climbs up and sits on the kitchen counter. 'Even if people are from another country, they don't have to speak another language do they?'

I begin chopping a tomato. 'How d'you mean?'

'I mean, if someone comes here from another country, they can still speak English, can't they? They don't have to speak African?'

'Well. Plenty of people from Africa speak English. And there isn't just one African language. They speak French in lots of Africa.'

'Some people are a bit like the Germans though, aren't they? They think that only certain people can be German. But in England.'

'Erm. How do you –'

'Like, how they said you had to have blonde hair and blue eyes if you wanted to live in Germany.'

'You mean the Nazis? In the Second World War?'

'We read a story about the war at school. The Germans are bad.'

'Well, yes, I mean, no –'

I hear the front door open and Max slides off the

counter and runs into the hall. 'Dad! Guess what happened today!'

Down the street there is an allotment scheme. It was set up by Dan's ex – Max's mother – who is a community activist. She applied for funding, built raised beds and set up a cooking evening in the local community centre called *From Estate to Plate*. The beds are wild and fertile, with rhubarb and chard nestling among the coriander that has gone to seed. I sometimes help Dan do a bit of weeding out there.

'Veg and the pursuit of the good life,' he says. 'She was all about putting principles into practice.'

My grandad had grown vegetables too. But his principles, his idea of the good life would have been different. He grew them for perhaps three reasons: because he knew how to; to feed his family; and to show that they were not idle good-for-nothings like the other families on the estate.

When he came over from Ireland, he removed the concrete slabs in the yard at the back of his council house and dug it up to make a vegetable patch. Against the fence, he built a small greenhouse for tomatoes and he collected rainwater in big blue barrels. He used to walk Sinead and me up and down the path that ran through his crops, testing us on the names of things.

In our search for a flat to rent, we walk around many rooms, looking out of many windows. From some you can see pink roses, lush trees and borders of primrose and pansy; from others, squat grey pebble-dash houses with washing hanging out to dry. We smile as letting agents talk at us and then we walk home. Sometimes we walk home down the street with two William Hills and a Bet Fred. Sometimes past the low concrete precinct with a Chinese and a chippy. Sometimes past the beautifully lit café that sells sourdough bread and the shop that sells nothing but greetings cards and scented candles. As we walk, we argue about whatever flat we have just seen:

'I liked it.'

'It has damp.'

'That's because it's a hundred years old.'

'We don't want to live in a damp flat.'

'But the bedroom had a lovely view of that old tree –'

'I'm not moving into a flat that's full of damp. It doesn't matter how beautiful it looks, love.'

That's when I say, don't call me *love*, and the tone of the argument shifts. Sometimes he rolls his eyes and says that I know he doesn't mean anything by it; sometimes he says sorry, you know I don't mean it like that. I say what I always say: I don't care how you mean it, use my fucking name.

One weekend we go to a party a few streets down. Like at Dan's, the close and staircase are dark and peeling, lined with cracked tiles and exposed concrete. The door to the flat is open and, inside, it smells of dog and weed. Young-ish people, wearing jumpers and no make-up, one with dreadlocks, sit on the floor and around a large table. Some-one with a big smile offers us a glass of nettle stout. We take jars and fill them up from a plastic vat with a tap on the side, the liquid bubbling and dark.

'It's enormous. Like a factory. Or an abattoir.'

The man in the gold sparkly top has a weathered face

and he is older than his skinniness led me to assume from the back. He tells me he considers himself to be culturally Catholic and that I shouldn't go into any of the pubs around this way. He tells me about the other, bigger Louden Tavern, right next door to the stadium.

'I can hear their singing through my bedroom window and do you know what the cunts are singing?'

As he leans over to refill his jar he sings it: '*Your famine is over, why don't you go home.*'

The penultimate flat we see is just south of the city centre. The owner, a South Asian man with an oversized suit and salesman patter, lets us in. He takes us up the dark tenement staircase to the flat.

'The tenants are out. Take your time. Look around.'

In the hall, wires are sticking out of the walls, and in the kitchen the lino is rotting. The bathroom door is locked and taped shut. In the bedroom there are two bare single mattresses on the floor. Next to one is a pair of flip-flops and folded up on each is a fleece blanket, the kind you see packed into transparent plastic suitcases on market stalls, wild wolf or lion scenes printed onto them. In the lounge, glass is missing from one of the windows. Two mugs and a plate sit in the middle of the otherwise empty room. There are no signs of any other possessions.

'Have the tenants moved out?'

'No, no. They have lived here for six months. From Afghanistan.' He sees us looking at the broken window. 'Yes, I need to make many repairs. But, I'm so busy, it is difficult to arrange, you know?'

W hen we were packing to move north, Tom was going through a box of his old things and in it there was a bottle-green felt cap, the size of my hand. It was clumped in dust, its lining torn and its mustard piping hanging loose. The Cub Scout insignia on the front had almost completely faded away.

Why a conker, I had asked Tom, that evening after his trip to Sri Lanka. He had laughed shyly.

'I don't know why I said that.'

'You must have had a reason.'

I watched his face and saw him decide to be brave.

'Because of the shininess. It's so shiny that it looks like it's wet, but when you touch it it's firm. That's what conkers are like.'

Cunt as conker. Tom's passwords were actually the opposite of shibboleths; they confirmed him not as a member of my tribe, but as someone new. They were proof of difference, proof that there was a real-life other person in there, behind his eyes.

Tom comes to meet me at Wonderworld, the children's play centre where I work, and we walk home with our bikes. The area is full of half-built blocks of luxury flats, their fronts still to be added. Tall towers of concrete layers, metal poles holding the floors apart.

Calling me love, I explain again, is like when they used to call me *twin*. Twin was all they'd ever call us at school. Like it made no difference at all which one we were. Tom says, Fine. Fine, but it's damp and I'm not living in a damp flat again. I think of the first flat we lived in, back in

London. It was damp and above a fried chicken shop. In that flat, I used to wake up in the night panicking – 'Move over. Move over. You're squashing me. You're taking up all the space!' – and force Tom to the very edge of the bed. The greasy smell of frying flesh, and always the clattering of metal, trays or knives or whatever it was, clattering all around us late into the night.

We cross the road where the pavement has been cordoned off by a construction site.

'Also, I need to find a way of not being afraid of Max,' I say.

'Yes.'

'It's like I hate in children all the things I hold important for people in general.'

'Like what?'

'A sense of themselves, the audacity to express their desires. You know. There is something about kids believing that what they have to say is important, thinking of *themselves* as important, that makes me crazy.' I watch Tom steer his bike around the lamp-post with one hand before I carry on. 'And you know how dogs can smell your fear? I worry kids can smell how fake I am.'

'I don't even know what that means. You're not fake.'

'Then why do I feel like this?'

All those stories and films and cartoons where people find themselves trapped in other realms, where they get frozen or where their reflections step out of a mirror. Children know all about fakes. They get it because they know how it feels to look out through a turned-to-stone figure's eyes; they know that if you do what the grown-ups want you will get the love, but also that you'll keep getting stuck inside. Stuck looking out through the eye holes of the person you have to pretend to be to get it.

As we cycle along past the Asda, we pass a bus stop advertising Coke Zero: zero sugar; zero calories.

'So, what the fuck is in it?' I shout into the wind.

T he pieces of cake smell like glue. I find them wrapped in serviettes between the sofa and the bottom shelf of the bookcase. They are in a plastic bag full of our childhood photos, gathered up and forgotten after my cousin's hen do the month before. It reminds me of a spell I once read about, a Colombian *liga*: twist together a toasted mixture of your own armpit hair and one of his pubes and put them next to his picture overnight. Add the hairs to his coffee the next morning to stop him leaving. Other possible ingredients were toenails, semen, excrement and spittle.

'It's weird that we didn't smell it till now,' Tom says.

I can never remember whether it's serviette or napkin that's meant to indicate poshness. Dad always noticed these things in people. Where do piece-of-tissue, paper towel or blue roll fit in? I just need something to wrap my slice of *Sugar Vegetable Oils Fortified Wheat Flour Powdered Egg Glucose Syrup Wheat Starch Humectant-Maize Starch-Tapioca Starch-Raising Agents (Diphosphates, Potassium Carbonates, Sodium Carbonates) Colours Emulsifier (Mono- and Diglycerides of Fatty Acids) Preservative (Potassium Sorbate) Acidity Regulator (Citric Acid) Glazing Agent (Beeswax) Skimmed Milk Powder Flavouring* in.

At what point exactly does cake become something other than cake?

The reason I'm even looking down between the sofa and the bookcase is to find the jigsaw that I got as a secret Santa present from work. It's a *Gone with the Wind* jigsaw puzzle – Scarlett and Rhett kissing, with wagons burning in the distance. I want to show it to Alice, who is visiting, the bump of baby number two showing.

'A small glass is fine, right?'

'I'm sure it's fine.'

'The answer is different depending where you look. And it seems to change every couple of years.'

'Tom's mum drank and smoked through all her pregnancies and he's fine. My mum did neither and –'

We laugh.

I met Alice when I was at art college twelve years ago, and we lived together for a while when I was nineteen. The day I moved in, in the kitchen of the little flat that belonged to an aunt of hers, she said: I want us to live –

She stopped to find the perfect word. I had just piled all my binbags into my new room and she was spooning limeflower tea into a vintage teapot. Bright low light was coming through the old sash window and I watched her take two china teacups from her shelf.

'I want us to live – aspirationally.'

We didn't realise, when we first met, that we were exotic to one another. She was beautiful, moving in a cloud of expensive scent and exquisite fabric. Back then, I suppose, we all floated somewhat, sauntering back to our student halls, oblivious to the cars and late-night screams of the red-light district. But she floated higher than most. When she described me as free, she won me over straight away; free was exactly what I wasn't, but what I desperately wanted to be. It was only later that I realised that, by free, she meant something about being ignorant of a certain set of rules, free from knowing how things ought to be done. Free as something novel and as something to do with class.

When Alice's first daughter, Wren, was nearly a year old, she used to put everything in her mouth. All the crumbs or bits of dirt she found on the floor. She also had a way of opening her mouth very very wide when she saw something she liked; she would stretch it open as if she was trying to look through it, as if she believed the whole world could be hers if she could just *get it in there*.

I open the old jigsaw box.

'If I could find someone to do it for me, I could get it glued together and stick it up above the dresser. But I'd have to watch the film first.'

'Why?'

'Why what?'

'Why do you have to see the film before you can stick it up on your wall?'

'Because of course I do. You can sum a person up entirely with the line she has posters on her wall of films she's never seen.'

Aspirationally. I remember the sick shift in my stomach as

I marshalled my excuses. I looked around her little sitting room: the Degas postcards and the pale peony in a jam jar. I think I just pretended she hadn't said it. I drank my lime-flower tea and smiled.

'This is great tea. What did you say it was again?'

Alice leans over and pours more wine. 'Why can't you just do the puzzle yourself?'

I shrugged. 'I hate jigsaw puzzles. Such a waste of time. What would it say about my life if I had the time to put all thousand pieces together?'

I was dating Chloe while I lived at Alice's. Letters would arrive by post, written on brown paper in her tiny floral handwriting. On my break at the restaurant in the afternoon, I would go out the back to read the latest. I wiped aside wet cigarette butts and sat on the step, leftover rain dripping from the top of the bin shed onto the empty cans of cooking oil. Along with one letter, Chloe had copied out a poem by Keats: *Thou still unravish'd bride of quietness, Thou foster-child of silence and slow time.*

Sometimes, apropos of nothing, the oil cans boomed. Chloe's writing was small and I could feel the cold concrete getting colder through my trousers. I moved down the poem, trying to take it in. *What mad pursuit, What struggle to escape?* I skimmed to the end: *Beauty is truth, truth beauty – that is all ye know on earth, and all ye need to know.* The words sat like grape pips on my tongue: they made me want to spit.

Sex as escape, they say, love as return. The familiar, with its draw and its repulsion. People were admiring when we first got together. There was a sense that I was brave, woke, a defier of convention. I took the praise, it would have been churlish not to; other people's words, other people's worlds, can be much easier to live inside than your own. Whatever it was that I needed to come out as, come out of, was something I could forget all about in the softness of Chloe's lips, the way she brushed my hair back from my face, the feeling of being loved.

We first kissed sitting by the edge of a river with a curved brick bridge across it. There was no wind and in the flat surface of the water the arch of the bridge turned full circle.

'How was your granny?'

My grandmother was ill and I had just been to visit her. I shrugged. 'Okay, I guess.'

'Are you close?'

'I don't know.'

'You don't know?'

'Yeah. And maybe I don't feel like making small talk about my family.'

Chloe shrugged back. 'So, don't. Talk as big as you like.'

'Fine, I will. How's your granny?'

'Dead.'

The night I met her, a few weeks before, she'd asked me whether I believed in God; some comment about my childhood must have prompted her to check. At my inde-cision, my refusal to outright deny his existence, she asked for my address. A few days later, a book arrived with her phone number inside it. Dawkins' *The Blind Watchmaker*. I read it over the weekend and that's how we became friends.

Once we got together, we'd walk down the street, holding hands and talking. I'd ask myself: but what is it that I'm faking? Then sometimes, for the sake of variety, I'd change the wording: but what is it that I'm lying *about*?

I found myself saying such stupid things when the boats started sinking in the Mediterranean. Hundreds were dying every week. Four hundred off the coast of Libya, six hundred and fifty off the coast of Lampedusa. Stupid things like, I can't believe we aren't doing more. I can't believe we're not helping. As if Europe is the good guy in some global blockbuster; as if people do the right thing and life is fair. The European Council has drawn up a scheme to take in refugees, but it's voluntary. Hungary is building a razor-wire fence along its border with Serbia, Bulgaria along its border with Turkey, Macedonia along its border with Greece.

Just to do something, I start volunteering once a week at a night shelter. It's in a church underneath the M8 and has been set up for homeless asylum seekers. The first night I visited, the manager showed me around.

'This is where the men sleep.'

It was a scuffed parquet-floored hall with a raised stage at the front. He showed me a cupboard at the back with thirty or so foam mattresses stacked on their sides and beside them bundles of sheets and sleeping bags tied up with string. 'Guests are very particular about which blankets they use. It can become a cause of conflict.'

He took me to the kitchen.

'How long do people generally stay?' I asked.

'Some have been here for over a year.' He stood a mop back up against the wall. 'Others only stay a night or two. They want to move on. Of course they do. They want to move on to better things. What I always say is this: you can't prevent movement – only increase or lessen the violence that goes with it.'

Last week I sat in the shelter's TV room and watched the BBC news. Obama, in high-definition orange, was giving his speech at the Democratic convention for the 2016 US elections, but the captions lagged whole scenes behind the words. The men made tea, strummed an out-of-tune guitar and wandered about. The room smelt of unwashed bedding, body odour and bravado. In the corner, someone snored loudly.

'All night like that. Louis!'

'Louis!'

The snorer jerked awake, grinned and closed his eyes again. On the TV, Obama hugged Hillary Clinton.

The day we finally move into our new flat in Govan Hill, forty more migrants drown off the coast of Sicily. On our first night there, we go down to the next street along to get falafel. It's a Kurdish kebab shop and they give us free lentil soup while we wait. It is delicious and the colour of custard.

'I drank my first cocktail at a bar in an old custard

factory,' I tell Tom. He asks what I think the definition of a cocktail is.

'More than just spirit and mixer?'

'Two different kinds of alcohol?'

'Or is it to do with the kind of glass?'

We are pleased with ourselves, finding a shop nearby that does such good falafel.

'Birmingham is the birthplace of custard powder,' I tell him.

'No shit.'

'Yep. Invented because Alfred Bird's wife was allergic to eggs.'

Kids from everywhere play outside in our new area. Little girls shriek and crouch behind parked cars and little boys chase them. Later, the boys cross the road to watch the teenagers kick a ball in a dead-end street. The Bangladeshi grocer on the corner keeps coming out to shoo them away.

'Gipsy kids. Always in here trying to take things. No manners.'

'Is that right?' I am squeezing his red peppers, looking for one that isn't too wrinkled. I put my can of coconut milk on the counter with the best pepper I can find. 'They can't all be like that.'

'Then you try running a shop around here.'

After we have been living in the new flat for a few weeks, a friend whose sister's husband is a police officer tells us that the next street along is notorious for holding trafficked girls in sexual slavery. Falafel and that group of boys eating crisps and hitting a scaffolding pole with a stick; falafel and that woman carrying the enormous bag of rice, falafel and all those closed doors and curtained windows.

V itrines lined the corridors on the way in to the biology department where Chloe worked. She was assisting with an experiment at the university lab, changing the water for a group of frogs, cleaning their tanks and recording their behaviour. I used to go and see her sometimes, when I had a split shift at the restaurant; she'd move between the benches in her white lab coat while I ate my sandwiches and watched.

Her job was to record how the amphibians responded to the changes in light. With the tank lids on, the tadpoles were black in colour, but with them off, under the light, they turned pale and translucent. In the play of the afternoon sun, the mass of bodies in the tanks under the window would ripple, changing colour with the movement of the clouds. When I asked her why they changed, she said it was a kind of camouflage. They were adapting to their environment as a form of self-preservation.

All the way down the corridor to her lab, the glass-fronted shelves displayed jarred specimens: some held butterflies and others coiled sea flora and labelled stones. Some were stranger, containing lizards or mice, paws poised, eyes staring. There was a whole shelf of embryonic creatures, eyeless and goat-like, packed in so tight that their folded skin was pressed up against the glass, bodies shaped by its curve. Further down the corridor were fish skeletons and twisted octopi, then after that were the brains: wrinkled, pickled and preserved in all their maggoty glory.

It was after about six months of dating that Chloe ordered us a dildo. It arrived in a white cardboard box and was a fluorescent-purple shade of plastic.

'It wasn't that colour online,' she said as I took off her tights. 'It was definitely more of a flesh colour in the picture.'

I was lying on top when I began to push it inside her. She was smiling and then she closed her eyes. It was only when she cried out suddenly, as if in pain, that I found myself getting wetter. This must be why they like it, I thought, pushing the dildo further inside her as she cried out again.

I am walking into town and there is a man with two dogs walking in front of me. The dogs are scrawny and thin, one on either side of him. He looks homeless and battered; juggling sticks poking out of the top of his old rucksack. He is holding both dogs very tightly by their leads and each time one seems as if it wants to move, he pulls the lead hard and winds it once more round his hand. I follow him all the way to the river, listening to him bark at the dogs to behave, tightening and winding until he has both fists right next to their taut, twisted necks.

It was like that time, a few months ago, going down the steps to Kelvinhall subway: there was a ginger fox tail sticking out of the jeans of the man in front of me. The tail was alert, rising up from the base and flourishing into a fall. I followed it down the stairs and along the platform. I guess you don't get to choose what turns you on. Chloe used to wear her hair in a ponytail sometimes and it had the same effect: girlish, but also that tension of the upward bit before the fall, the sense of something swishing around buttocks. What turns you on, what reminds you of something else, you don't get to choose that shit. The tail's owner had a handlebar moustache and leather jacket. *Please stand back. The train is approaching.* People began putting phones in pockets and picking up bags. He stood, watching the tracks, and in the gust of hot air his tail shimmied.

That night, in bed, Tom had moved in to kiss me and I had pulled back.

'What would you say if I said I liked tails?'

'Like, *like* them, like them?'

'Yeah.'

'I'd say we have a tiger suit with a tail somewhere. That one Dan wore at Glastonbury.'

'No. Not a onesie.'

'It's with all the camping stuff.'

'Not an outfit. Just a tail.'

'Okay. I'd say okay and I'll bear it in mind. But I'd also say, let's not try to run before we can walk.'

'It's different now. You're different now.'

Tom is chopping onions. He can chop them into really fine slices. I cry when I chop onions, so I have to

31

do it fast, making fat, uneven chunks. The radio is on and saying that support is increasing for the Republican candidate, Donald Trump.

'So, you think I should go?'

'I'm not saying you should go,' he says. 'I'm just saying that you *could* go. You underestimate yourself when you say you don't think you'll be able to handle it.'

Sinead is in Glasgow for an art festival and wants to meet up for a drink. I take Tom's advice and, when I get to the restaurant, she's already there. I watch her pretend not to watch me as I walk towards her.

When I get to the table, I lean over and hug her shoulder blade.

'Nice top.'

She looks down at herself. 'Yeah, a friend was throwing out a load of stuff and I got this.'

She is nervous. Her face, as always, a mask of mine.

The first usage of the word *skeuomorph* was by Dr Henry Colley March in 1889: *the transfer of thong-work from the flint axe, where it was functional, to the bronze celt, where it was skeuomorphic.* His point was this: to make a prehistoric axe you had to use a strip of animal hide to tie a wooden handle to a sharpened piece of flint. Later, when such a tool could be fashioned out of bronze, and even though they had no function at all, markings imitating the thong wrapping were still added.

The counter at our All You Can Eat Vegan Asian Buffet is lined with silver trays: noodles, rice, broccoli, peppers and other unidentifiable coloured objects. The dim fluorescent strip hanging over the counter gives the food a lacquered shine. It's been over a year since we last met.

Skeuo as container or tool; *morph* as form or shape. I'm trying to work out if a skeuomorph is the opposite of an isomorph. An isomorph is an arrangement in which the relations and proportions between elements are preserved, a structure that doesn't alter its fundamental form as it grows. I decide they are not opposites; they are more like different kinds of sameness, fake sameness and real sameness. Isomorphs can look different but be the same deep down, but with a skeuomorph the sameness is only ever superficial – a copy caught up in a past it no longer even remembers.

We fill our plates and sit back down. On top of my rice, in a deep red sauce, I have a pile of fake shrimps. Eyes, antennae and shell all in place. Sinead has noodles, with brown strips in a thick black sauce.

'Let me try a vegan prawn.' She picks one off my plate and puts it in her mouth. 'What do you think it is?'

'Hard to say. Starch and gum?' I bite into one. 'Lots of sugar.'

'Yeah.'

'So, how's it going?'

'Okay. I think.' Sinead nods slowly as she eats. 'I've been internet dating.'

'Yeah? How's that going?'

'I'm seeing one of them again. On Thursday. He's into spanking.'

'How do you know?'

'It was all over his profile. We met and it was all we talked about. All night. It was wonderful, actually. For the first time I could say what I really wanted. What I actually, really wanted. And I realised that that's why it disgusts me and makes me so angry when men come on to me. It's because I know they just want sex. They are like' – she strokes my thigh under the table – 'and I'm like, get the fuck away from me. And it's because I don't want what they want. I just want that. Just that. It's like as if I was gay – I'm not gay, I don't like women at all – but it's like that. Like, I'm looking for a totally different event. And, he's hot. He's a banker. I'm just worried I'll fall too in love with him.'

'Where are you going to meet him?'

'His house.'

'Is that wise?'

'Of all of the men I met, he was definitely the most sane. I'd definitely recommend spanking for you guys.'

'What? Why?'

'I think it'd be good for you.'

'Right.'

'What?'

'Nothing. Let's just move on.'

'What, I can't talk about it anymore?'

'Let's just talk about something else for a bit.'

'What, because it makes you feel uncomfortable, I can't talk about it?'

'We have been talking about it. Now I want to talk about something else.'

'You're not the only one here, you know. Why do you

get to decide what we talk about? I can talk about whatever I like.'

'I don't want to talk about it anymore.'

'Why are you being so controlling?'

'I'm not being controlling, I'm just –'

We've been here before. Sinead calls me a fascist. I tell her to fuck off. She tells me I need therapy. I tell her to fuck off. Under the strip lights, her skin is pale and pored; mine must look exactly the same.

According to the Oxford Dictionary, the skeuomorph is *an object or feature which imitates the design of a similar artefact made from another material.* For something to be a skeuomorph, a trait inherent in the material construction of the original object must remain, even when the object is made using a different method or substance. A skeuomorph, then, is an example not of fakery, but of material metaphor; it is when a visual detail, once the result of material necessity, now does, or *is*, something else.

We are quiet again, drinking our bottles of beer.

'So, is the sex good with Tom?'

I look down as I wrap noodles around my chopsticks. 'Yeah. Although, sometimes it's hard.'

'That's good, no?'

'Ha.'

'How is it hard?'

'I don't know. You know. Something to do with us. I get – panicky.'

She is nodding as she eats. 'That's why Tinder is so

good. It's all so straight-up. You can clarify right at the start whether there's going to be sex or not. Takes all the bullshit out of it.'

'Is it Stephen Fry who has that line, if God didn't want us to eat animals, he wouldn't have made them out of meat?'

'Wasn't that Eddie Izzard? But, Tom seems okay. Like, if you were on the streets or something, he'd move over and share his flattened box with you.'

'Why do you say that?'

'What?'

'About us being out on the street?'

'Well, I mean, he seems like the kind of man who, like, if you were desperate, he'd help you out.'

Pale and porey and looking at me like she knows I know exactly what she means.

'I'm not desperate. And I don't want it to be about him helping me out.'

'Oh. Well, what d'you want it to be about?'

'About love.'

'Right.'

'Don't say that like that.'

'Like what?'

'Like I'm an idiot.'

'Well, you did just say *love* like it was something nice. Or something we'd all recognise on a shelf like a hat.'

'Fine. I want it to be about moving forward, then.'

'Right.'

'Why can't it be about that?'

'You tell me.'

'Everything isn't the past, you know. Everything doesn't

have to always be like it was. This is different.'

'Sure. Great. I agree. The two of you can both just be normal and sorted and fine. Whatever you want.'

'Right.' I drink my beer and watch a woman in high-waisted leather trousers come out of the toilets and return to her table. 'So, tell me more about your dating.'

'I think it's really good for me. All of my therapists have said that one of my problems is that I'm so afraid of everything.'

'Really? I didn't think –'

'I know you don't. But anyway. They say I avoid things.'

Sitting out the back at the restaurant where I used to work, I'd listen to the melody made from ground surface variation as old rain dripped from the roof gutters. I'd sit on the step near the covered area for the wheelie bins, where soggy cardboard boxes were piled up around those empty cooking oil cans. The rain was dull and loud on the plastic bin lids, almost soundless on the cardboard and high-pitched and echoing on the tin. Alongside the drips was the sudden boom of the cans. Maybe percussion, maybe trapped gas, maybe a memory. BOOM.

We fill our plates up again. Skewers of something and skeuomorphic crispy duck.

'What came first, the fake chicken or the eggless omelette?'

'I hate puns,' Sinead says.

'It's not even a pun.'

'Clever clever and usually unfunny.'

'It's not a pun, it's –'

'I hate that chicken and egg shit. It's that shit that I get into when I think about us. There's no egg without a chicken but yadda, yadda. If it weren't for that etcetera, etcetera, but then if it weren't for that, etcetera. And what? No one is responsible? No one is to blame?'

'To blame for what?'

'What the fuck is wrong with you? How do you manage to –'

'Let's not.'

'Oh right. Here it comes. *Let's not talk about that.*'

'Well, let's not. It never goes well.'

'Because you never let us talk about it.'

'I just –'

'Refuse.

'Yes. I refuse to –'

'To what?'

'To be sucked into –'

'What? Sucked into what?'

'This shit.'

'My shit?'

'Yes. Your shit.'

'Nothing to do with you?'

'I don't want –'

'What? You don't want what?'

I'm cycling past that bridge again. In an evening writing class, a few years after I saw that car roll into the river, I handed in a story about it. The tutor – a woman in her fifties who wore too much velvet – told me it didn't really work. It was unrealistic, she said.

'I don't believe that none of the characters would have jumped in. Surely, someone would jump in.'

I lock my bike up and open Wonderworld. I lift the shutters, turn off the alarm, let the cleaners in and tidy up the craft area. In the office upstairs, I make coffee, turn on my computer and open Facebook. A Canadian woman I used to half know, who now has impossibly cute kids, has posted what she cooked them for dinner: kale with some kind of buckwheat pancakes. Someone from art college, now a fashion photographer, has posted more heavily filtered shots of beautiful women. Someone we met in Turkey and drank tequila-flavoured beer with has posted a picture of herself at a protest and something in Turkish. I order supplies, check the staff rota and read the news. I look up prices for individually wrapped cake, wipe-clean bunting and wholesale make-your-own finger puppet kits. I look at an overhead shot of black people squashed onto the deck of a rusted blue ship, a photo of far too many people on a sinking dingy and photos of a dead body on a beach. I read about dire predictions for the economy if we Brexit, about rioting at a migrant camp on Lesbos and how a Syrian migrant has been shot trying to cross the Slovak-Hungarian border. Strains of *If You're Happy and You Know It, Clap Your Hands* float up the stairs – the morning storytelling session is starting. I switch back to Facebook. Someone has shared a Vote Leave ad about Turkey. On a red background are the words *Population 76 million. Joining the EU.* Is that even true? I'm typing the words *Turkey joining* in the search bar when my radio buzzes and someone speaks: Supervisor to lower ground. Code two.

I get the tub of Urine-Dry powder then take the lift down to the basement. On the lower floor we have a pretend beach play area with miniature child-sized deckchairs and fake ice creams. Two girls are bouncing a beach ball and a woman is hissing, poking her finger in a small boy's face while he cries. I shake blue powder over the puddle on the blue plastic waves and tell them it's not a problem.

'It is a problem,' she says. 'He does it on purpose. He does it to make me look bad.'

In the lift on the way back up to the office, in order not to think about the little boy and his mother, I think about when we used Dan's projector to look at the Blue Mosque. Tom's brother had emailed to say he was going to Istanbul and that he wanted recommendations. We attached Dan's mini-projector to our laptop and went back there, the streets of Cihangir filling the wall in Google Maps' street view.

'What about that café where we had the amazing breakfast?'

Tom moved the cursor and the scene shifted. 'I remember that shop!'

'Where was the breakfast place?'

'Do you think we can get inside the Blue Mosque?'

'I wouldn't think so.'

Tom went back into map view and pulled out, then found Sultanahmet Square and zoomed back in. You could go inside, and we did: curved white walls and the high-domed blue ceiling. The bulbs in a low-hanging chandelier distorted by flash photography, people sitting on a red carpet underneath geometric stained glass. There were people on their own, praying or looking at their phones, and also what looked like a school group. Then we saw the man whose legs had become detached from his body – tracksuit bottoms with a stripe down the side, fading away at the top, then five feet away, his large torso, floating legless in a leather jacket.

'Look at him!'

Tom changed our viewing position and the scene swooped around. Stone pillars and a roof painted with a dark red script; polished benches and an ornate wooden lattice. Then the top half of a security guard, his crisp epauletted shirt layered over a woman in a pink headscarf, each of them facing in opposite directions. Unreality caught and stored.

That afternoon Jackie, who works in the schools outreach team, shows me the new marketing software they are using. It's a heat map of customer activity on our website. The areas that are the deepest red show where teachers or parents have spent the most time, and the blue or green patches show where there has been least engagement.

'They get a bit lost, then they find *About Us*, then they go to either *Opening Times* or *What's On*. Then, mostly, they leave,' Jackie says.

A set of red blotches that fade to orange then yellow, turning green and dimming back to blue near the edge of the screen. The image is almost symmetrical, like a painting folded in two, or like one of those old ink-blot tests.

It was Jackie who told me about Mosaic. It's a system run by Experian, the company our letting agent had used to do a credit check on us. It uses *sophisticated consumer data analysis* to produce what it calls *a comprehensive cross-channel segmentation*, splitting the population up into 15 groups and 66 types. The types were called things like *Suburban Mindsets* and *Careers and Kids*, but also things like *Claimant Cultures*. I was shocked by the literalness, the way they felt like they could just go ahead and *name* things.

Group O was *Liberal Opinion*, and within it, type O63 was *Urban Cool*. Group J was *Claimant Cultures*, with J42 as *Worn-out Workers*, and J44 as *New Parents in Need*. Group A was *Alpha Territory*, with A02 as *Voices of Authority* and A04 as *Serious Money*. Typical names are also given for each segment: for *Municipal Dependency* it's Wayne and Leanne, for *Suburban Comfort* it's Geoffrey and Valerie.

Later in the afternoon when I look up those ink-blot tests, I find the transcript of an interview with Dr Rorschach himself. On the first card, he says, his patients usually see a bat or a butterfly. On the second, a friendly gnome or two elephants, reaching out to one another. Card five is most commonly seen as a musical instrument or a moth. He explains his scoring system: *It's not so much about what they imagine they see, but rather how much of the ink blot they use to come to a decision: do they use the whole image or just part of it? I am interested in observing how hard the viewer will work to make sense of the whole scene, I am interested in observing how he deals with conflictual information.*

Sinead and I gave ink-blot paintings to Mum on Mother's Day one year. At school, we were told to fold a piece of paper in half, then open it out and paint only on one side, with plenty of paint and in any pattern that we liked. The old shirts we brought in for art class were buttoned up backwards to protect our gingham uniforms as we dabbed away, the teacher walking among us:

'Good, good.'

'No, now that's silly. You've used far too much paint. You're going to need to start that again.'

'Yes, yes, don't be too stingy with the paint there.'

After a while the next instruction was given: 'Very, very carefully fold your paper back over again and smooth it down.' She watched us do this. 'Now, open it back up.'

Mum sat up in bed with the toast and tea we'd helped Dad make and looked at the pictures.

'Aren't these lovely?'

'What do you think they are, what do you think they are?'

'Well, I think they're butterflies. Beautiful colourful butterflies.'

We shake our heads.

I visited Sinead in the November of her first term at art school. We went to a party in a terraced Victorian house with fairy lights wound through the staircase banisters. There was a bath full of very strong punch and an ill-defined fancy dress theme. I lost Sinead and was wandering around, nodding as politely as I could when people exclaimed in excitement at our visual resemblance, and fending off people who refused to believe they did not know me. I went upstairs, but the queue for the toilet was too long, and I carried on down the landing to nose around in the bedrooms. Inside the first door, a guy had his jeans and boxers around his ankles and a girl was sitting on top of a chest of drawers, legs wrapped around his waist. It was Sinead. Her eyes were closed, her hair was in disarray, and she was moaning. I closed the door.

That Christmas, when we were eighteen, she gave me a stranger than usual present. We were in the front room, wrapping paper on the carpet, the tree in the corner by the TV. The present was a wooden seesaw on a string. There was a small wooden doll at each end and, if you pulled it along, they moved up and down.

'Zero-sum,' she said as I opened it. 'I saw it in a charity shop and I thought, that's perfect.'

T om reaches over and strokes my hair. One of my favourite stories about Tom is the one where he cries at Christmas: he is five or six and his great-aunt has made him a Super Ted doll – buttons for eyes, a red felt cape and the fire emblem stitched onto his front. He is crying because, even though he knows Super Ted isn't real, he also knows that this isn't the real Super Ted.

Sinead sitting on the floor between Dad's feet, her face a mask of mine. As children, we would wait, wet hair against the radiator, for Dad to blow-dry us.

'Look how lovely and silky your hair is now. Look how lovely and silky her hair is now.'

Warm air, the slow stroke of the brush, the sense of watching and being watched at the same time.

'Say what you see. Just say what you see.'

Catch Phrase's Roy Walker encouraged us as we ate our tea on Saturday evenings. The contestants on the telly trying to decipher the clues and fragments flashing across the pixelated screen. *Just say what you see*: peas, chips and Findus crispy pancakes. Ketchup and two identical girls shouting out their near-identical guesses.

As Tom rests his hand on the top of my head and pushes my hair behind my ear there is a thick buzzing, like electrical feedback or static. This noise fills my mind and cannot be thought through. All I can do, if I try really hard, is withstand it and remain in place.

D ziga Vertov's *Man with a Movie Camera* was showing on my first shift.

This film represents
AN EXPERIMENTATION IN COMMUNICATION
WITHOUT THE USE OF PLOT
WITHOUT THE HELP OF SCENES
WITHOUT THE HELP OF CHARACTER

That's what it said at the start of the screening, in an old-fashioned font on a title card. Then there were montages of factories lines and switchboards, cigarettes rolling off conveyor belts and trams silently colliding. Random repeating sequences, cameras filming other

cameras. I ushered the film five times. I'd never seen anything like it.

I began working at the small arts cinema the summer
after the Christmas Sinead gave me the seesaw. I took the
tickets on the door and sat at the back during the screening in case of an emergency. After the film, I turned on the
lights and opened the doors. That was also the summer
that Sinead went into hospital. I used to watch the audi-
ence's faces carefully as I turned up the lights and afterwards, as I picked popcorn off the carpet, I would think
about all that hope. How I had seen it fade as the lights
rose; how I'd seen it become dangerous again, disavowed,
now that there was no longer anywhere safe to put it.

That summer, I also worked at Iceland Frozen Foods
Supermarket. At the cinema, I tore tickets at the screen
door and watched strange foreign films and at the supermarket, I sat on the checkout and watched shopping roll
down the conveyor belts towards me. Frozen pies, frozen
peas, frozen pizza. Chicken nuggets, Viennetta, potato
waffles. I beeped them all through the till.

On my third viewing of *Man with a Movie Camera*, Roger,
who worked in the box office, told me that the woman you
see cutting up strips of film was Vertov's wife.

'She edited most of his work. And that's her, cutting
up the very film we are watching and hanging it over the
light box.'

Later, I read that theorists called Vertov's work 'data-
base cinema': *no beginning or end; no development – the-
matically, formally or otherwise – which would organise their
elements into a sequence. Instead, collections of individual*

items, where every item has the same significance as any other.

That summer was also the summer that I sawed a doll off the seesaw with a bread knife.

W alter Benjamin describes *fragments of a vessel which must match one another in the smallest detail, although they need not be like one another.* He writes of an ancient belief that a vessel, made to hold God's holy force, was broken, shards of it spreading across the world. Humanity's task, according to this doctrine, is to uncover these fragments and piece them back together. A matching of hidden resemblances, a reading of correspondences between dissimilar things, a seeing of sameness with something beyond the senses.

The baby rats snuggle up, the milk passing through their translucent stomachs. These rats are taking part in an experiment into the workings of glucocorticoid receptor genes. A mischief is their collective noun. I'm watching a video of them on YouTube, the mother rat licking her litter, some stomachs turning whiter than others. As she licks furless flesh, her tongue moves along the spine of each pup, making pleats of skin bunch up at their necks. Lick distribution is sporadic and haphazard, the still-blind mischief burrowing and climbing over one another, trying to find a spot in the warmth.

It was more than ten years ago when I first read about the rat experiment. I'm surprised that I still remember the lead scientist's strange name. I search *moshe szyf genes rats* while I'm at work and watch some of the clips that come up. I first read about it in Birmingham Library when I was eighteen. It was only now, with the boats sinking in the Med and seeing those pictures of life jackets on the shore, that I'd started thinking about it again. That furry pile of blind luck and chance.

I had found the original article in a serious looking magazine called something like *Proceedings of the Royal Society of Biological Sciences*. It was there that I first read the word *epigenetics*. I wasn't used to reading scientific literature; my understanding of science had ended before it ever really started, copying out an image of the cross section of a leaf while Ben McKlusky once again filled his Adidas sports bag with gas from the Bunsen burner then lit it with a lighter. I don't know why I picked that journal up and opened it. The typeface was small and awkward. I don't remember the title of the article, but I remember the first line; after all the names and dates and credentials it said *Abstract: Early experience permanently alters behaviour and psychology*. The shock and then the words I could understand floating up from the mass that I couldn't: *programming, rat offspring licking, first week of life, persist into adulthood, alter DNA structure*. I closed the journal and returned it to where I'd found it. What crazy truths were these, written in this strange parenthesis-filled code?

The gist, I now know, was this: rats are born with their glucocorticoid receptor genes switched off and it is literally the mother's licks that switches these genes on. The NR3C1 gene is found in the hippocampus of

48

both rats and humans and is altered in both by different levels of early care. These chemical alterations then go on to determine the body's ability to regulate stress and inflammatory responses, affecting the entire immune system.

After watching the rat videos at work, I play a TED talk with the epigeneticist Courtney Griffin. She has twin girls and says that before her daughters were born she would have put her money on nature over nurture. She struts across the stage saying, *I kind of half-jokingly started to wonder what the consequences would be, if we just sent one twin to day care and maybe just kind of tucked the other one in my office drawer during the workday. Despite their identical DNA, I somehow doubted that things would turn out all that well for the twin in the office drawer.* I lean over and switch her off.

You know when, as someone is talking, you think of the perfect next thing to say – a joke, an ironic line, something completely context-dependent? You hold it on your tongue and wait for the speaker to take a breath. Then, as they do, someone else says just what you were going to say, but better?

Chipped blue toenail varnish and those open drawers with other people's things hanging out. Her legs wrapped around his back. The paleness of her thin arm on his shoulder, the slight wobble of her bicep. Gasping as if totally unwatched, as if the whole world belonged to her.

Something foreclosed before it even began. Something

destined forever to be nothing but a copy, a repeat. Sometimes, when I remember that image of her having sex at the party, Sinead looks right at me. Other times she doesn't see me at all. I don't know which is worse.

T om and I talk again about having children as we drive to Portobello beach. When we get there, we walk along past the seaside shops and discuss how we don't have the money or the stability to raise a family and that we seem to be no longer having sex. On the beach, we peel off our shoes and socks and sit on the sand. Behind us, four our old men are getting drunk in a graffitied pavilion with Greek-style columns. In the water, one deflated pink armband drifts as the waves roll in and out. Beyond it, in the distance, there is the green mound of an island. Tom thinks it is the isle of Inchkeith.

Tom's gran passed away two weeks ago and he tells me that, when his mum was clearing out her house, she found a handwritten list of collective nouns folded inside one of her cookery books. A murmuration of starlings. A shrewdness of apes. An unkindness of ravens.

'Mum said she wasn't sure they were all legit.'

A knot of toads. A pitying of doves. He also tells me about how his grandmother threw his mum out for a while when she was eighteen and pregnant with him. I tell him about a story I'd just read in the news, about Turkish police raiding a makeshift factory. They had found thousands of fake life jackets, neon orange vests stuffed with cardboard and sponge instead of proper foam.

Despite the wind, children in their underwear are

shrieking at the water's edge. The large women who sit watching them are solid to the point of making movement look unnatural.

'We are not a graceful people,' Tom says.

On the first Christmas he spent with my family, as he sat at the kitchen table showing my dad how to download an app onto his new phone, Tom says he sensed me coming into the room. He told me later that he had reached out his hand without looking, to touch my leg as I passed, but when he looked up, it was her. He said we must give off the same energy or something; that there must be something alike in us, other than our mannerisms or appearance – something more like an aura.

On our first date, he told me about a *Star Trek*-based thought experiment known as the Teleportation Paradox. I hadn't heard of it.

'The question is, if we go into a teleportation device and our bodies are transported, atom by atom, to a distant location, are we still the same person when we get out at the other end?'

'Hmm.'

'Some completely identical physical body is now somewhere else. Is it a replica, or is it us?'

I take a sip of my beer. 'What about the minds?'

'Well, that's it. Are our bodies and minds really distinct from one another? If the body is replicated, does that mean our mind will be replicated too? Or is it that there is no *real* us anyway – no *I* at all?'

'I like that.'

'And if there is no *real* us –'

'There is no *I* to go missing in the teleporter.'

I invited him back to mine that first night and he cycled standing up while I sat on the seat with my feet dangling. I held his hot T-shirted chest through the wind of passing takeaways and pound shops, then he sat on my sofa while I made us a drink.

'What is it?'

'Campari. It's all there is. I think it used to be cool in the 70s.'

He held up the half-pint glass and looked at it. 'Is this how they drank it?'

I sat. 'They probably added ice.'

'So, there is more about that teleporter that I didn't tell you,' he said, moving closer.

'Okay.'

'One day it goes wrong. Usually the original is destroyed once he's made somewhere else, but this time he doesn't get destroyed. He is just left there, standing inside the teleporter where he went in, and the other one, the one that got recreated in the new location, has climbed out and is getting on with his day. So, the question is this: which one should the secret teleporter police destroy?'

'Do they have to destroy one?'

'Something about doppelgängers. The universe will explode if they meet.'

'I have to say which they should kill?'

'Yeah.'

'I don't know. You tell me.'

'Well, the argument I like best is the one where they destroy the original: he's no longer the most valid version of himself, so he has to go.'

He looked at me carefully for my response when he said that. I offered a big smile. The newer man, he reiterated, is the realer one. Then he leaned in and kissed me.

On the beach, we watch litter whirling up out of the bin. One of the mothers shouts to her child: Get here. I said, get here now. When it starts to get cold, we put on our socks.

A t the night shelter, we cook from out-of-date food that local supermarkets drop off. Each item carries a sticker saying *Unfit for Human Consumption*. I am making veggie chilli and Josh, another volunteer, is chopping carrots and sliding them into the pan. Taha is preparing the rice, after explaining to me why I don't do it right. I first met Taha when I sat next to him in the TV room. He asked if I was a new volunteer and then, gesturing to the other men that a joke was on its way, asked: So, what do you think? I'm a fake refugee or a real refugee?

When I tell Taha that I have moved house he asks if the new place is a house or a flat.

'Flat.'

'How many bedrooms?'

'Two.'

'Too many small flats in this country. In Sudan, I had a house. A big, big house with a big garden.' He shows with his hands how big and how much distance there was between his house and the next one. 'Very big. Very big. Not like a flat.'

I add more paprika to the chilli and wish there was enough cultural overlap to reference the Brummie from Harry Enfield.

Later, I sit beside Mikal and watch TV. There are more homeless Eastern Europeans staying these days. On the table, a plate of donated Danish swirls are hardening. Mikal bites into one, pastry flaking down his T-shirt.

'I had a job, but I was fired. In a factory. We were smoking cigarettes outside on the break, but two men were smoking weed. They say, all of you go. All of us lose our job.'

'That seems unfair.'

'Yes. Now I am homeless. I go to the job centre and look for jobs. I am waiting to hear about – what do you call it – the money?'

'Benefits?'

'Yes. I am waiting to hear.'

The TV is showing an advert for Lidl.

'Ha. We packed meat for them,' Mikal says. 'My factory packed for Lidl, Tesco and Marks & Spencer. All same meat, different packagings.'

There have been some incidents and a growing number of complaints. A meeting for representatives from the local community has been called. Volunteers can attend, but not the men living at the shelter. People from the nearby estate sit in rows and a councillor and a church governor sit behind a table at the front. The church governor begins, but is shouted down.

'Who are you, anyway? We never see you round here. You don't know anything about what it's like.'

Someone else interrupts: 'What I want to know is, why is this being dumped on us, just like everything else? We don't want strangers hanging around at all hours of the night. Would you want that in your area?'

A woman in a green T-shirt stands up. 'You know, just because this place is a shithole – doesn't mean you can dump all this on us.'

The comment gets a round of applause. By the end of the meeting a compromise of sorts is reached. In order to protect the local primary school children from coming into contact with strangers, all asylum-seeking men must be off church property by 8 a.m. They can then not return to the area until 8 p.m. As I and a few of the other volunteers get up to leave, a local woman turns to us:

'And why is this not a space for us? Where are all you *volunteers* when *we* need you? You're all hypocrites. Who gives a shit about the community who actually live round here?'

Outside the train window, the cows are sitting. The hills are misted, the trees faded silhouettes. Sheep don't sit when rain is coming; in the next field along they are still scattered, grazing or wandering slowly, lambs trotting in a line behind their mother. In another field, a bit further along, some cows are sitting while others stand, the future still undecided.

I'm on my way to London. In my book, Dr Lisa Feldman Barrett says that our brain uses the past to continually create and revise a mental model of the world. She says that *there is the real of an atom or a molecule, of a quark or a Higgs boson, but there is also another kind of real, one that is completely dependent on human observers.* All that real needs to come into being is for a couple of people to agree on something and give it a name.

There is a video clip that I watched last month and I want to rewatch. I search for *Baltimore riots mother* on my phone and find it. I hadn't realised until today that #*Heromom* and #*motheroftheyear* had gone viral. The clip was filmed on someone's mobile during the Freddie Gray riots in Baltimore. I watch a street with broken windows, burnt-out cars and a line of riot police. Young black men, with scarves covering their mouths, are chanting, hands up, don't shoot. People are throwing things at the police and shouting. Suddenly, a large African-American woman, wearing a yellow jumpsuit and gold jewellery, marches on to the screen. She yells, *Get over here, get the fuck over here*, then grabs a teenage boy and whacks him twice around the head. He backs away, half covering his head, and she whacks him again. He puts his hands up, dodges, and she whacks him once more. Then she turns and walks away, him following her, moving down the street, away from the crowd. Violence to stop violence about violence, because, as the governor had said to applause in a speech the day before, violence will not be tolerated.

There are also the Venetian millefiori beads that I saw years ago at the Victoria and Albert Museum. They are small, brightly coloured glass beads that look a bit like marbles, and each one with a flower or a swirl or a star suspended inside it. They work in the same way as a stick of sugar rock, the motif – *I love Blackpool* – running through the whole cane so that if it is chopped up into individual boiled sweets, the words remain imprinted on each one.

Millefiori beads used to be taken to Africa and swapped for slaves; stolen men, women and children were then swapped for textiles, rum and sugar. Alongside this, a way of making fake millefiori – or *kiffa* beads – developed in West Africa: bottles, cans, twigs and other detritus were ground up and mixed with saliva, then heated and shaped into canes that could be sliced up for beads. Later, in the 60s, travelling hippies bought and renamed these trinkets *love beads;* they wore strings of them to express their desire to live in a world undistorted by capitalist consumption. I'm trying to work out which are the skeuomorphs and which are the isomorphs in this story.

The train has stopped. There are sidings with brown freight trolleys in them. The scene looks like the photograph Conrad Waddington used, back in the 50s, to explain how epigenetics worked. It was a black and white photo of a snowy Cambridgeshire train yard, a single track dividing around a wooden signal hut, then branching out into a dozen more forking paths, boxcars and wagons lined up on some and not others, switch mechanisms tapering the rails as they crossed one another. Waddington also sometimes used a sketch of an uneven hill, winding channels and paths running down it and, at the top, a ball waiting to roll. Sinead had emailed me. Did I want to come to London and meet at the Tate, to go and see the Diane

Arbus retrospective. It is two months since we met up at the Asian buffet. She said there were some things she wanted to talk about. I emailed back and said okay.

Your heart rate, blood pressure, cortisol levels and breathing fluctuate. But these muscle movements and changes are only instances of emotion if you categorise them in that way. Without the concepts, they don't exist, and there are only moving faces, beating hearts and circulating hormones. I put the book down again.

Moon in the white sky. Stark black pylons, wire, grey boxes and dark green shrubs. It is early morning now and the sleeper train is rolling past a high concave wall, the tips of stone crosses and tombs rising above it. My back is twisted from sleeping on an upright seat. Lichen covers brick and the train enters a tunnel. My pale reflection staring blankly back at me.

There was a cave that Tom and I visited on our holiday to Turkey. The rock all around was the pale pink of strawberry ice cream and inside the cave it was damp and mostly dark, except for a thin strip of sunlight from a hole in the wall. On the back wall, twelve tall men were painted in a richly coloured, life-sized row. Solemn and elegant, in robes of bright reds and oranges, they were holding chalices, grapes and bread. It was a shock, as I walked towards them, to see that their features had been scrubbed off, and that their expressions were nothing but the blank pink surface of the rock. Blank like my face is now in the black window.

S inead and I walk through the polished hallway to buy tickets for the exhibition. We walk silently past a sign for the Turner room. When we were ten, our uncle dropped us off and we spent the whole day in there, looking at the seascapes.

And the –

Yeah!

And the –

Yes. And the –

Oh!

Our elbows were beside each other like they always were, thin forearms dangling and crossed. That day we read the plaque about how Turner tied himself to the mast of a ship during a snowstorm; he had wanted to feel the spray on his face as the boat sailed the high waters, to feel it, so he could paint it. We looked at the painting of a tiny boat in a storming sea and we loved him, loved him for communicating it all without any words at all.

It's so –

That he –

I wish –

And me.

We went back to the Tate two years later. Sinead was skipping – 'Let's go to the Turner room!' – and smiling her new smile; the one that stretched her lips to cover the brace I didn't have. The new smile that didn't look like a smile at all. We walked around the edge of the room, looking at each painting, but I was careful now not to let our elbows touch. The paintings were all still the same, the same swirls and the same colours, but this time, instead of being pictures of everything, they were more like pictures of nothing.

Sinead used to have a poster of John Lennon on her wall when we were teenagers. It was black and white with the line *Either I exist, or the other people exist; it can't be both* along the bottom. But now, when I look online, I can't find any reference to the quote. There was definitely a poster of him in her room. Maybe that line was just something she used to say when she was standing in her doorway next to the poster. Or maybe it was something I used to think while she was standing there.

When I visited the Turners myself in the years after I left home, I developed a different theory about what had made his paintings feel so real. I'd stand back and look at *Slave Ship* or *Shipwreck* across the room, the stormy sea, the boats, the waves, and all the tiny people, running, jumping and trying to escape. Then I'd go up close and look again. Nothing but smears and splodges of paint. The people were both there and not there at the same time, and that was what did it: blink and other people fade to nothing at all.

One time I looked for the picture of the tiny boat at sea and the plaque with the story about the mast. The picture was still there but the plaque had been replaced: there was a new blurb now, detailing how Turner's younger sister had died of cholera and how Turner himself had been committed to a mental asylum. A note at the bottom read: *It is famously said that Turner conceived this image while lashed to the mast of a ship during an actual storm at sea. This story seems, however, to be nothing more than myth.*

Sinead and I go into the Arbus exhibition. The photographs are black and white and mostly from the 1960s. They are pictures of strippers, carnival performers, nudists, dwarfs, members of the LGBTQ+ community and twins. There is a quote from Arbus included in an introduction on the wall: *Freaks were a thing I photographed a lot. There's a quality of legend about freaks. Like a person in a fairy tale who stops you and demands that you answer a riddle. Most people go through life dreading they'll have a traumatic experience. Freaks were born with their trauma. They've already passed their test in life.*

'Do you think that's true?' I ask Sinead. She lifts a finger to her lips and shakes her head, beckons for me to follow her.

Russian midgets, a man in curlers, a nudist couple watching TV at home. A Mexican dwarf, a swan in front of a Disneyland castle, a boy in a suit wearing a badge that says BOMB HANOI and giant at home with his parents in the Bronx. There are fragments of quotes from critics printed in large text on the wall above the pictures. Susan Sontag: *Arbus photographs people who are pathetic, pitiable and repulsive from a vantage point based on distance and privilege. She seeks out subjects considered to be disreputable, taboo or marginal. Her view is always from the outside.*

A woman on a floral sofa holding a baby monkey wearing a bonnet. A child crying, tears and spit dripping from his face. When we reach a photograph of two identical twins, Sinead stops. Two girls, about seven, are in identical dark dresses with oversized lace collars. Their bulbous eyes are staring straight at the camera, one half smiling, the other not.

I turn to move on, but Sinead takes hold of my arm.

'I thought this would be a good place for us to discuss reparations.'

II

The impressive bunch of flowers on her kitchen table is not unlike Alice herself; artfully arranged and extraordinarily tasteful, sprigs of vintage white lace between petals of purple and orange silk. She'll know their Latin names too.

'They're beautiful.'

'Thank you. I picked them from the garden.'

Rose is in her highchair and Wren, who is three, is eating a piece of cucumber. Richard is at the hob, heating up a pan of soup. I'm not sure how well Richard and I get on; I think that if he was asked to describe me in one word, he'd use the word *quirky*.

We sit around the table and eat. Richard holds out an apple and speaks to Wren in Welsh. I survey the shelf of small, labelled Kilner jars to the left of his head: ancho chilli, black cumin, nigella seeds and a small tub of something yellow, fluffy and unlabelled.

'Did you hear that? *Ydych chi am afal hwn?*'

Wren smiles shyly. *'Ie!'*

Richard hands her the apple. 'Alice! She's getting it! I asked her if she wanted the apple and she said the right yes.'

Alice is coaxing Rose to eat another spoon of carrot purée. *'Merch dda*, Wren. Good girl!'

Wren bites into her apple.

'That's why it's so difficult to learn,' Richard tells me. He has been taking Welsh lessons at the local school. 'There isn't a single word for yes or no – the right answer depends on the type of question.'

'That's interesting. How do you work it out?'

'Oh, there's a whole range of things – the tense, whether its singular or plural, the status of who you are talking to – No, Wren. Put that away.'

Alice is sticking out her tongue at baby Rose, who returns the gesture. Wren has done the same, leaving her tongue hanging out as she shouts:

'Mummy! Look!'

'Wren, you're not a baby,' Richard tells her.

'I want hot tea. Mummy, I want hot tea.'

'Not right now, darling.' Alice turns to me. 'That's what she's always asking for these days. It means she wants to use the coffee maker to steam milk.'

The espresso machine in the corner is all sleek metal and black; Richard had shown Wren how it worked while Alice was recovering from Rose's birth. A low stool is positioned near the counter and Wren is often to be found kneeling on it, admiring the machine's gleaming silver magic.

'But I need hot tea now.'

Richard shakes his head. 'No, Wren. Enough with the milk already.'

Richard goes to his Welsh class and I offer to cook while Alice does bath time. There is a large butternut squash on the counter and when I poke around inside their fridge I find some yogurt and half a carton of tomato passata. I tear the leaves off what is left of a parsley plant and chop garlic.

The kitchen is like a picture-book kitchen; the shelves and table are rustic hardwood and on the counter there are lilac sweet peas in a milk bottle. Outside the window, the stretch of the lawn – and the trees and stream beyond it – are darkening. I put onion on to fry and add fennel seeds and paprika. Upstairs, I can hear Wren resisting. Blu-tacked to the wall is one of her pictures, red and orange, the wax thick with scribbling. I add a little bit of each chilli and a pinch of the unnamed yellow fluff. Upstairs, Wren is telling Alice to read it again and I can hear her sing-song intonation as she begins to repeat the story. I lay the butternut squash on the wooden chopping board and slice it in half, leaning in on both sides of the knife to get through the skin. The halves roll apart and show their pale orange flesh. Something is wrong. There are no seeds.

After dinner, the three of us go into the sitting room.

'It's not really Wales here, though,' Richard is saying.

Alice retorts that of course it is.

'It's a border town.'

'In *Wales*.'

'But it's not proper Wales – not like Cyfarthfa or Dow-lais. It doesn't have that industrial history.'

'It's a market town.'

'Except the market is closing.'

Alice turns to me. 'They are building a Morrisons where the market used to be.'

Richard is from the Home Counties but has been

reading all about Welsh history since he started going to his classes. He seems to still find time to read, Alice had told me on the phone, while I can't even string a sentence together. She decided that Richard – who lived on her street and knew friends of hers – was the One when she left a bowl Coxes from her garden on his doorstep, and he turned up on hers that very evening with a freshly baked upside-down apple cake. They told this anecdote at their wedding a year later.

Once, after they were first married and Alice was pregnant, I went for a drink with Richard. He talked about the five languages of love: words, gifts, acts of service, touch and time – how it was all about using the right language for each particular person at the right time. Back at their flat, he stopped outside the front door. If we go in and she's ironing my shirts, he said, then I'll know she loves me. I think he was serious. We found Alice curled up on the sofa, sewing a new button onto her coat.

The last time I visited, Rose was only a few days old. Wren, bewildered and betrayed, was downstairs with her dad. That must have been when he taught her to steam the milk. Alice was in bed in one of Richard's shirts, crying gently as she breastfed. Rose's open mouth searching and sucking, her eyes closed tight. Alice laughed a little.

'Can you imagine ever being so small?'

I had held the tiny sleeping animal, feeling the fierce heat beneath her skin and thinking about the ambiguity of the Welsh affirmative as I moved my head.

Do I remember being that small is a big question. Like two bags of sugar, Dad used to say. Two pounds each.

Before we were rushed off to the incubator, he had held us both just for a second, one in the palm of each hand. There is a photo I think, or have I just been told the story so many times that I can see it? Dad grinning, a tiny baby, blue and bloody, in each palm. Surely we were too ill for that? Did Mum even get a hold? Alice took Rose back from me and talked about skin-to-skin.

'It's amazing how it regulates their nervous system.'

The image that came to me was from a film. I can't remember which. A scene in a strip club where one of the strippers puts the man's face – he was a boy really, this was some kind of coming-of-age gift – between her breasts and jiggled. His whole head was in there, and when she released him he looked like a baby, dazed and drunk.

Do I remember ever being that small? Sinead and I were in neonatal care for our first two months, the two of us top and tail in an incubator, wired up, machines and tubes doing the work of skin-to-skin. No one could touch us at all for fear of infection.

Mum says we had our own language right from the start. We used to talk to each other in our cot. She said that a few weeks after they took us home, she came into the bedroom one morning and we were lying on our sides touching each other's faces. Baby's don't usually do that, she said. They don't turn and face one another, they ignore each other. And with babies that young, usually their arms only flail and grab, but we were stroking each other's faces so intentionally, so gently. Murmuring and making these cooey sounds.

In the morning, as we eat porridge and toast, Wren climbs

onto her mother, trying to get wherever Rose already is. Alice pulls the breastfeeding baby further in towards herself, shifting her thigh as she tries to make more space on her lap.

'Gently, Wren, gently.'

Wren is pulling at Alice's shirt, trying to get in on the action. 'No love, you don't need booby milk anymore. You're a big girl now.'

Wren is getting upset, pushing at Alice's breast and at Rose. Alice shifts again, moving Rose to the side, out of her reach. She wraps her free arm around Wren, trying to take hold of her hands.

'Hey! Wren, look!' I say, putting a mug on top of my head and pulling a stupid face. Wren keeps crying and pulling at her mother's shirt. As Alice shouts for Richard, Rose starts, falls off the nipple and begins to cry as well.

The cow on the sticker, on the foil triangle, is wearing earrings. The earrings are Laughing Cow cheese triangles and, on those earrings, that cow is also wearing Laughing Cow cheese triangle earrings as well. Sinead and I could talk about the cow on the cow on the cow for hours when we were six or seven and camping, eating only cheese triangles, baguettes and ice cream. Laughing ourselves silly into the *mise en abyme*.

It was on one of those holidays that we met a French girl in a red swimming costume in the Eurocamp playground. The next morning, we went knocking on the nearby tents. Working out how such knocking might be achieved was the first hurdle; the canvas slumped when it met with fist, so we decided one of us would hold it firm while the other made the noiseless rap.

A sudden impatient face: *'Bonjour?'*

Our only French line: *'Par lay vou ang lais?'*

We were strategic, we decided that if we could find the French for *stop*, we could answer yes to the girl's invitation to play. We could then use that word if she made the seesaw go too high, bumped it down too hard, or became in any other way problematic. After asking at three different tents, we found a woman who spoke English. She told us that the word we were looking for was *Arrêtes*. We shouted *Merci* and ran back to the playground. We both knew about the way a game could suddenly take you like a big wave, dragging you under; and how, without the right words to find the other's hand and swim back up again, you'd both be left under the water, swallowing in the roar, the stinging salt filling your nose. At seven, we already knew that you needed a safe-word before you started anything.

As Sinead and I had stood in front of Diane Arbus's twins, she told me in more detail about the night she ended up in hospital. As she told me again what had happened – she was watching TV, *Friends*, and then, the next thing she knew, she was in hospital and we were all there around her bed. She watched my face carefully, her eyes locked onto mine.

'Now you tell me,' she said. 'What were you doing that night?'

The very first time I visited Alice's grandparents' house, I was eighteen. Alice's grandmother had recently passed away and Alice had promised her mother she would go and check on things. We lay on the lawn, ate Welsh cakes and slept in the attic that is now Wren's bedroom. The next day, we walked across heather and hills to a small dwelling that her great-grandfather had built into the side of the rock.

Alice made a fire in the stone pit near the entrance and we brought the cushions from the old sofa outside with a bottle of red wine and two mugs. After half a mug, I told her.

'My sister went into hospital last week.'

'Is she okay? What happened?'

My stomach hurt. A tightening, a twisting. What happened. What happened to put Sinead in hospital. How could I answer that? How could I even think it? Start somewhere. Find a fact and start there. The doctor. Doctors know facts.

'The doctor said that her heart just stopped. At first they thought it was an overdose. But they couldn't find any drugs in her system. She was basically dead. They restarted her heart on the way to the hospital.'

'Oh my God.'

'It happened the other Friday. The night we were at the pub.'

'The night you disappeared off?'

'Yeah.'

'Who was that guy?'

'Just a guy. A guy I know. We –' I wrapped my coat more tightly around myself. My brain didn't seem to be supplying my mouth with any more words. Alice was shaking her head, dismissing her own question, her eyes concerned.

'How is she now?

I looked up at the stars. I couldn't tell Alice about the test. If she knew how fucked up I really was, she definitely wouldn't want to be friends anymore. And she was all I had really. Mum and Dad had already thought there was something wrong with us, that general stench of disappointment – and now it was official. The guy. I guess I could talk about that. That was a story people understood. Cheating and stealing another girl's man. Hadn't there been a story like that with the twins on *Neighbours*?

'I knew the guy through Sinead.' Or, put another way: I'd seen her legs wrapped around his naked back at that party.

'Did you get together?'

'Yeah.'

It was the first time I'd ever come. Then the phone ringing early in the morning. I'd already been awake for about an hour. The enormity of being in bed beside a boy. The smell of him, the smell of his sheets – the smell of real life. I was in; I was in like she was in, in on the inside where real life happened. I was looking at his stubble, looking at each individual black strand and how it came out of his chin through its own tiny hole, how his T-shirt was wrinkled up around the shoulders, and how inside that T-shirt there was his body. Warm and smelling like a real-life boy's body. I answered the phone without looking who it was. I didn't want him to wake yet; I didn't know what the next bit was and I didn't want it to start before I'd worked it out.

71

Mum's voice. I moved silently towards the kitchen in his flat and whispered hello.

'Siobhan. It's Sinead. She's in hospital.'

I felt my body feel it. Like when you see the keys you couldn't find on the side of the bath and then remember taking them out of your back pocket before you sat down on the toilet. *Ah yes, of course.* I felt my body recognise and understand a familiar causal logic. I could smell cheap plastic feathers singeing.

'It was my first time,' I told Alice. 'Then, in the morning, my mum rang to say Sinead was in hospital.'

'Oh, wow. How horrid. And your first time too. Was it okay?'

'A bit weird.'

I cried all the way through it. Silent tears that started and wouldn't stop. They started the moment Adam touched the skin across my ribs. His large hands so gentle. Touching my skin like he knew it, like he loved it. A longing, but not the lustful longing you read about or see in films. Not like how they say it is at all, but everything drowned out by an ache that filled my whole body. Then there was the moment where I was sat on top of him, the sound of traffic outside his window and strains of *I'll be there for you* coming from another room. He was touching me somewhere I had never been touched before and I was melting. The thawing, aching pain in my throat, between my legs and in my hips. And those hot tears all the way through. 'But it was good. I think.'

'Is your sister okay?'

When Mum and Dad went out to speak to the specialist, I asked Sinead what had happened. She was sitting up in the hospital bed. When she shrugged, the stand that she was attached to by a tube wobbled. She said she was at her friend Jess's house. They were both completely sober and watching *Friends* on TV. The last thing she remembered was the episode ending and Jess reaching over to turn it off.

'The doctors are worried about her test results,' I told Alice. 'They want Mum and Dad to watch out for signs. Mum and Dad want me to watch out for them too.'

Sinead had gone off to another room to take the test and left Mum, Dad and me in her room. I was sat on the side of the bed, Mum was looking out of the window into the car park and Dad was standing beside the chair.

'I knew all this Fine Art nonsense was a mistake. If she's into drugs or something, you need to tell us.'

'Why are you making out like this is somehow my fault?'

'This isn't the kind of thing that just happens. Not in any normal family. She must have taken something, done something.'

'How should I know?'

Mum turned around to face me. 'Do you do drugs? Are we going to get a call in a few months' time about you?'

After Sinead came back, they went out to talk to the doctor again and I stayed in the room with her. She sat down next to me in her pale green hospital gown, her white pants showing where it fell open. She was excited.

'The test was crazy. The questions are crazy!'

As she started to tell me about the questions, I could feel the room getting hotter.

'Is that radiator on? It's so hot in here.' I stood up. 'Do these windows open?'

'What? I don't know. Are you listening? This test is how they decide whether people are crazy or not – and the test itself is crazy! Like, one of the questions is something like, can you read other people's minds or can other people read yours. Another is about not knowing what to say or if what you do say sounds strange. *Incoherent*, it said. Like, do you sometimes know what other people are thinking? I mean, we do! All the time! And do people not understand us? All the time! There was one about feeling your thoughts interrupted or seeing things that other people can't.'

Outside the window, there was a family walking to their car. A girl with crutches and one leg in a cast, hobbling beside her parents. The dad was opening the door, the mum helping her into the passenger seat, taking her crutches and putting them in the boot.

'Siobhan!'

I turned back to face her. 'This was the test? These were the questions on the test?'

'Yes! It's like a test to see if you are mad or suicidal or something, and I'm there answering *yes, definitely* to all of them!' She laughed. 'It's like a test to see if you are us!'

Alice is wrapped in a thick orange blanket, holding her mug with both hands. 'What kind of signs?'

'Oh, just the usual, I guess.

You need to look out for strange behaviours, Mum said. Those strange ways of thinking that the doctor was talking about. Dad said, you know how you two sometimes get – then just left the sentence hanging there. We all knew what he meant, anyway. And I knew that they meant for me to watch out for them in myself as well. I could feel something in them moving further away as they said it. *You know how you two get.* Sinead and I on one side, them and everyone else on the other.

A few days later, I went to the new internet café near the library to see if I could find out some more about the test. I found something called STEPI, a Schizophrenia Test and Early Psychosis Indicator. There was a list of questions: *1) I have trouble speaking the words I want to say and people have told me that what I say is incoherent. 2) I see or hear things that other people cannot see or hear. 3) I think other people can sometimes read my mind, or I can read other minds. 4) I sometimes have trouble distinguishing whether something I experience or perceive may be real or may only be part of my imagination or my dreams.*

It was a test that had been used for a while in America and it was now being piloted here. It looked for clues, for early signs of future psychosis.

'Like the signs of a heart attack?' Alice asked.

'I guess.' I could feel her looking at me strangely, like something had shifted in her mind. 'Or just signs of, like, being weird. But that's just her. I'm fine. I mean, obviously. I mean, I don't get like that.'

Alice was watching the fire, the light passing over her face in a way that made it hard to read. I picked up a fat twig and started to peel off pieces of bark. I wanted Alice to say something. I could feel her thinking about how we were genetically identical. I could feel her backing away too. My stomach was twisting again. The bark was rotten and crumbling as I pulled at it. Oh, God. Now she was thinking about all the weird things I'd ever said, about that time I was trying to explain something about Sinead and I and the way we used to be, and I wasn't even making any sense. We were in a café and I was crying. She stayed completely quiet, waited until I'd finished, then asked if I wanted another tea. I felt her thinking about how crazy I was then, too.

'What? What are you thinking?' It came out louder than I meant it to. Alice turned, surprised.

'What do you mean? I'm thinking about what you're saying. About your sister.'

'Yeah. Well, look. It's all easy for you. You just get to be you. You don't have to keep explaining – people looking at you like you're –'

Incoherent. *Do you ever have trouble speaking the words you want to say – do people say you are incoherent –* Alice looked alarmed. 'Maybe you've drunk a bit too much wine?'

'Oh fuck off.'

Now she looked shocked, upset. 'I'm sorry about your sister, but I don't understand –'

'Forget it.' I turned away and watched the flames myself. Walk away. Just go.

'I don't mind talking about it, but –'

'I don't want to talk. Really. I don't. I just want to be by myself.'

'Okay then.' She stood up. 'I think I'll go to bed. I'll see you in the morning.'

I shifted closer to the fire, picked up the bottle and took a swig. Fine, go to bed. I don't need your shit. I made myself laugh out loud into the still black night. Sinead's laugh.

Sinead laughing as she recounted the test questions. It took her a while to notice I wasn't laughing with her. She was so sure we were together on this. Together against a world that didn't get it. But I could feel something changing, something becoming possible as she talked. She was still sitting on the side of the bed, her torso slightly twisted towards me as I stood at the window. Then her eyebrows furrowed slightly.

'What are you doing? Are you listening?'

I kept my face completely still. This is what *they* did, I realised. You just silently pulled back a little and slid something down over your eyes. I tried pulling back a little more. It was like a door, I realised, a silent, invisible, sliding door. And I was pulling it shut.

I drank more wine and picked up a new twig to peel. The fire was low and bluish now, only one log left to burn. I looked up at the stars and made myself shout out another laugh. How it felt to be astride Adam on the sofa, filling with all those right feelings, all the feelings a girl is meant to have while she sits on top of a man. I made myself look up at the stars and think about how free I was.

It was dawn when I woke beside the remains of the fire, my head on a sofa cushion, the orange woollen blanket spread over me. Alice must have brought it out after I fell asleep. The empty bottle of wine next to the pile of ash. I stood up, my hips stiff, keeping the blanket wrapped around me. The whole landscape was covered in mist. I started to walk, following a track along the side of the dwelling and then upwards, climbing steeply through trees and bramble until suddenly the trees stopped, the path turned and there was a clear view. The dips and crags of the valley swept below me, wide and green. My body took a breath in and I exhaled it out into the land that had unfurled before me. Yes. The important thing, more important than anything else, was to be sane.

W hen Tom first told me that he liked to go walking, I was sceptical.

'I don't get it.'

'It's great – you are in the outdoors, and when you get to the top of a mountain, you get the view . . .'

'That's what I don't get. The view. Standing at the top of a hill in the rain, looking at *the view*. What even is *a view*? I just don't get it. When I get to the top, to the *view*, I just think, I don't know what it means.'

Tom is a mapper for a medical NGO and he is always delighted to find a trig point, rubbing his fingers over the markings. The point is usually on a hilltop, a metal Y embedded in stone, sometimes with numerical markings engraved on it. When we come across one, he takes out his phone and checks the open-source digital map he is working on. If it's missing, he marks it on. A little stitch, connecting our particular spot to the global picture.

When he first showed me the website *what3words*, I was excited. We were in bed and he had the laptop on his lap.

'Every place in the world has three words to show where it is.' He entered our postcode. 'Look at the words we get.' The screen showed a map of Glasgow overlaid with a squared grid, our flat marked with a pin. In a red box three words had been generated to describe our location: blaze. events.forces.

We are in bed again. Our bent knees slotted through one another's as our bodies move closer. We kiss and then try, as we do, to find a path forwards, or back. Warm trails show themselves and then shift. I can hear his breathing and mine. He moves on top of me. I can see his pores and feel his weight, and then I can feel my fear. Pressure? Panic? Something else. I make myself keep kissing, keep running my hands down his back, through his hair. A feeling of being trapped. I push it away, move my pelvis up towards him and pull his tongue further into my mouth. He is hard and I can feel myself wanting him. At the same time my hips won't open. The feeling of being watched. I feel it even when we just hug. I meet my own eyes across the room as my head rests on his shoulder. I need him to get away from me. This isn't going to work.

We go walking in the Hidden Valley with our tent as autumn turns to winter. Trump is in. We are shocked but neither of us can find much to say about it. Last week, at the shelter, Samir had laughed and said, of course! He's a crazy fascist. Perfect for America.

The trees along the rocky path are beginning to turn orange and red. I think of the opening to Alistair Cooke's 1970s documentary, *Letters from America*, the camera panning over the colours of Vermont in the fall: *The beauty is deceptive as it cloaks the poorest, stoniest soil . . .*

The voice-over went on to describe how the bright

autumn colours were a side effect of poor soil, nothing more than a desperate bid for survival.

After our tent is up, we find a few branches to make a fire, then drink whisky and eat cheese. When the fire is close to burning out, we zip ourselves into our sleeping bags and lie outside next to it, putting together a list of sexual action points: I am to try to let things happen; he is to try to forget all the times I have rejected him. That's just me panicking, I explain again. It makes me panic.

'You need to trust me,' he says. 'I don't know what else to do.'

Early the next morning, while he is still asleep, I slip out of the tent and climb up the side of the valley. I climb until I begin to see the treetops on the other side. It is clear that something needs to be done about Tom and me. Down below I can see our lone tent, his small figure now moving around outside it, starting to pull out the pegs.

After he fell asleep last night, I lay in the tent and thought about what Richard had been telling me when I visited him and Alice. In the sitting room, after dinner, he told me what he'd been reading about the history of the Welsh language.

'Have you heard of the *Welsh Not*?'

I shook my head.

'It was used in Welsh schools, some say until as late as the 1940s. It was forbidden to speak Welsh and the *not* was usually some kind of stick that got given to any person heard speaking it. That person had to pass it on to anyone else they heard speaking Welsh. At the end of the day, whoever was left holding the stick would be beaten with it.'

He also told me that the tub of yellow fluff in the Kilner jar was bee pollen. He'd ordered it from a specialist online supplier.

'Allegedly, even a pinch contains all of the nutrients a human body needs to thrive. Vitamins, minerals, amino acids. All the good stuff.'

I sit on the rocky ground and watch the glorious red wash of self-preservation shimmering in the haze. When we first arrived in Glasgow, I washed Tom's little Cub Scout hat and put it in my sock drawer. Sometimes, when I imagine him wearing it, he is sitting at his parents' kitchen table watching a plump brown conker swell in a jar of vinegar; it has been gently baked in the oven overnight and by the end of the week it will be ready. Other times, he is walking along, feeling the pleasure of his own well-shone seed waiting warmly in his anorak pocket.

A trig point is a triangulation point and a triangulation system is a set-up that allows an unknown or unmarked position to be located if the co-ordinates of two other sites are known. Trig point, trigger point. When Tom touched me in a certain way, it triggered something. The danger of slippage. His hand on my head, in my hair, between my legs, and I would be slipping towards the space that was neither me nor him, the old void of slippage where I was neither me nor her, but us. That space between us where we used to live, where all was already known, but that was now gone. Or, he would touch me elsewhere and that would be different, but just as frightening: I was being touched while she was not. Tom; such luck would one day have to be paid for. Because if Sinead and I knew anything at all, it was that pleasure can only ever be stolen.

That the brain and the body respond to the past not the present – I already knew this. But now I knew it as a scientific fact. What was I supposed to do about the fact that the things I was supposed to enjoy were so frightening? That the amount of intimacy I needed to be able to bear to keep him was just too painful? Toast your own armpit hair and twist it together with one of his pubes. Add it to his coffee. Try not to think about it.

After Richard went to bed, Alice and I stayed up and drank wine. She pulled a wooden chair over to the radiator, putting the back of her head against it to help her hair dry.

'Do you remember that night we slept at your great-grandad's shelter?' I asked.

'Yeah. God. That feels like so long ago now.'

'You remember I was upset? I was telling you about Sinead?'

'She'd gone into hospital. I remember you slept outside on the ground by the fire.'

I watched the basil plant on the windowsill start to tremble as the washing machine quickened its spin. 'Do you think you're a kind person?'

Alice leant her head back. 'I think so. I try to be. I'm kind to my kids most of the time. I could probably be kinder to Richard.' She stared at the ceiling. 'Why do you ask that?'

'Like, if it came down to it. A hurricane, or a fire. Would

you save your family or yourself? If you had to choose?'
The basil pot rattled in its saucer and the multicoloured
bibs, baby-grows and T-shirts rose and fell in the rolling
drum. 'It's like that thing about crabs caught in a bucket,
how they climb up each other, trying to get to the top of
the pile and escape, but none of them can ever make it out
because the ones below drag them back down.'

'What is?'

'The clothes. Fighting away in there.'

Alice tipped her head between her knees and rubbed
the roots of her hair with her fingers. When she sat back
up, her hair was tousled and wild. 'I know I'd grab the
kids if there was danger. I wouldn't even think about it. I
wouldn't be able to leave them.'

'Do you think all mothers have that instinct? Is it hor-
monal? Chemical?'

'Chemical? Maybe. I'd be more likely to call it – I don't
know – *moral*.'

'You said you wouldn't even think about it. Can it be a
choice if you don't even think about it?'

'What are we actually talking about here?'

'Who can say? I'm reading a book about the brain. It's
by a Harvard neuroscientist. The real deal. And she argues
that every response or reaction we have is based on pre-
diction. Our brain receives input from the body about its
state, and asks, when did I last feel something like this?'

'Like what?'

'What I'm saying is that the brain only ever responds to
past situations. Your brain isn't ever responding to your
present situation at all – it's only ever responding to your
past. Only afterwards, *afterwards*, *after* it has prompted

whatever chemical or physical reaction and, even then, only if there's time, does it do something called error correction.'

Alice was looking out of the window, still running her fingers through her hair. 'Error correction?'

'That's when the brain compares the actual reality of the present situation with the one it predicted and responded to. It's crazy shit. *In everyday ordinary life our minds respond to a reality that isn't there.* This isn't art theory or psychoanalysis or something. This is brain scans and electrodes through the skull. This is *science. Proven neuroscience.*'

Alice wasn't really listening. And it didn't matter. The kitchen was warm and I sat back, looking at the homely mess of clothes and toys in the muted lamp light. On top of the dresser was a large stuffed rabbit and a small ballet slipper. How did she know how to do this, to create a home like this?

I thought of the photograph of the three circus ballerinas at the Arbus exhibition, two very fat and one tiny. Sinead walking on ahead, leading me towards the picture of the twins.

She was looking straight at me, still holding my arm.

'You took things that weren't yours to take. And you turned away when I needed you.'

'Oh, that's all so long ago now –'

'The fact it's in the past is irrelevant. You took things that weren't yours.'

'You're using a word, an idea, with such big historical connotations. I don't think it's appropriate –'

'Appropriate? What word? I want us to try and talk, to work things out –'

'You said *reparations*.'

'I didn't say that. I said *repairing things*.'

She was still holding on to my arm. And standing far too close to me, her eyes so like my own. She was lying. She didn't want repair, she wanted revenge.

W hen I woke up at Alice's the next morning, I lay in bed and listened to her dressing the children in the next room. Wren was giggling and it sounded like she had put her trousers on the wrong way round. I read about bee pollen on my phone. Bees collect pollen from plant stamens, mix it with secretions from their salivary glands, then place the mixture into pocket-like flaps on their hind legs. To obtain the pollen, a bee-keeper puts a kind of comb in the entrance of the hive to pull the flaps off as the bees enter. It is a practice widely condemned by wildlife charities; limbs, as well as pollen, routinely get torn off by the comb.

Sena, who cleaned Alice's house once a week, arrived at ten. She had recently returned from visiting her family in Turkey and that morning she was going to read our fortunes.

'My parents do it every time they have coffee. It's not like they believe in it exactly, it's just, how do you say – a ritual.' She was heating coffee, sugar and water in a blue pot she had brought back from Istanbul. It had a bulbous bottom and long elegant handle. I didn't feel good about this plan. Now was not a good time for me to be messing around with this kind of thing. As the coffee simmered, Sena arranged three sets of Alice's mismatched cups and saucers on the table. She laughed as she did it.

'They aren't the right cups. So the readings may not be *completely* true.'

The mimetic faculty, Walter Benjamin says, is a kind of sense-making. One that lets us *read what has never been written, a reading before all languages.* It is a way of understanding how one material – say, coffee grounds or tea leaves – is able to express something totally different from itself, to imitate or become something else. It is a way of noticing how *entrails, stars and dances* can speak of other things, a way of deciphering a forgotten, secret language. A torn chicken giblet lying across a wishbone on a plate, the alignment of Venus in the night sky, the shape as a dancer raises her arm then lifts her chin. There are hidden resemblances between things that do not, at first, seem connected – a web or pattern holding the microcosm and the macrocosm together, each detail whispering its connection to the whole.

In the months after what Mum called Sinead's *episode*, I spent a lot of time in the dark, on the top floor of Birmingham Central Library. I don't remember much about that time except that we were both back at home and I needed to be out of the house. I'd walk through the dim, musty-smelling reference section picking out books and opening them at random; sitting on the floor, reading a paragraph or two, then swapping books, letting one thing lead me on to the next. I learnt about footnotes and bibliographies and indexes. I knew nothing of disciplines and nothing of most of the things that I came across. I read like you might read a certain kind of poetry, riding the flow without following it, each word as random and worthwhile as any another. I had a small notebook where I jotted down things that seemed important. Clues and answers to questions I had no idea how to ask.

I first came upon the word *mimetic* in the science section, in a large *Oxford Dictionary of Earth Sciences*. I found T, then Tw, and there was an entry entitled *Twin Laws*. There was a slump of disappointment when I realised it was an entry about crystals. Something about mimetic twin crystals being more symmetrical than other crystals. This wasn't helpful, but I wrote the word down anyway. The next day I typed it into the catalogue, noted down the numbers and traced my finger along the spines.

Coloured spines, some tattered, some laminated. Often the book next to the one the Dewey Decimal Classification number suggested proved to be of more use. Animals, it turns out, use mimesis too; a weaker animal escapes a predator by pretending to be a stick or a leaf, or it frightens a hunter away by imitating something larger and more dangerous. The library stayed open into the evening and most nights I stayed until it closed, then got the bus home.

Birmingham Library was a massive brutalist block, its architectural style in keeping with our school and our local leisure centre: big, flat, utilitarian and ugly. There were concrete steps leading up to the automated entrance, doors that also led into a small mall with a McDonald's. An escalator took you past the open-plan children's area and up to the second floor, the light disappearing as you rose up into what was the very opposite of spires: enormous concrete blocks joined low false-ceiling tiles to the floor. At the top of the escalator, a bank of beige photocopiers hummed and behind them there were shelves of dark books and rows of tables. The desks were partitioned by blue screens in the style of office cubicles, grey plastic chairs tucked underneath them at intervals.

There was a computer in the far corner where you could search for things using a key word, author or title. It took a while for me to notice this and I spent a long time just walking between the aisles. The books were packed in tight, their numbered codes black on dark green, or white and sellotaped at the base of the spine.

I picked up many books, wandering around in the dark, but the first line I can remember writing down was from a book that was lying discarded on one of the desks. Its cover caught my eye – a strange soft pink shape and within it a winged topless woman, an octopus tentacle and a rearing horse all merging into one. *The Book of Imaginary Beings* by Jorge Luis Borges. I held it, looking more carefully at the cover: a hippopotamus with the snout of a pig, and the soft pink shape was a hand, gently holding the octopus. I opened it and read these words: *In advance of the invasion we will hear from the depths of mirrors the clatter of weapons.*

Yes. I found my pen. The whole piece was only a page long. It was called *The Fauna of Mirrors.* I wrote out the important bits: *In those days the world of mirrors and the world of men were not, as they are now, cut off from each other . . . you could come and go through mirrors. The Emperor . . .*

imprisoned them in their mirrors . . . he stripped them of their
power . . . Nonetheless, a day will come when the magic spell
will be shaken off. They will break through the barriers of
glass or metal and this time will not be defeated.

I put the word *twins* into the search box and set off to find
the suggested books, counting my way through the rows,
kneeling as I followed the decimals down to the floor. The
twin references were mostly journals detailing the medical and psychological results of studies using twins that
had been separated at birth and adopted. They were dry
and full of statistics, speaking not about the twins themselves but other technical things that were hard to follow.
I was also led to a book called *Children of the Flames*. This
was about Dr Mengele and his experiments on twins at
Auschwitz. I spent a few dark afternoons sitting on the
floor reading that.

'Oh darling, you can sit with me later. You've had your
lunch and now she's having hers. No, Wren, there
isn't room, my love.'

Alice told me that Wren had also started climbing into
Rose's Moses basket. She curled up in it, bowing the sides
and squashing the wicker, and would bleat and make crying sounds until Alice went and got her, picking her up
saying, There there, baby, don't cry.

After a few more thwarted attempts to get onto Alice's
lap, Wren stepped back from her mother and position-
ing herself directly in her eyeline, closed her eyes and
screamed as loudly as she could. Alice motioned for us
to keep talking over the screams. I asked Sena about her

trip and shouted that I'd also been to Turkey, and that I'd seen the caves in Cappadocia. She said she was sorry to hear that we had voted to leave the EU and that she didn't understand it. I shouted that I didn't understand it either. Eventually Wren stopped screaming and stood crying softly beside her mother. When Rose had finished feeding, Alice took them both upstairs for a nap.

I listened to Sena hoovering and thought about that summer in the library. There were false starts and dead ends, but slowly I found out that scapegoating and mimesis were connected. An introductory book about a French theorist called René Girard. I made a photocopy and underlined the important bits, making notes in the margins. Scapegoating was both the result of and the cure for mimetic rivalry. Desires were not spontaneous, but copied and competed over. These were finally words that spoke to the ones churning in my stomach. In my notebook, I wrote: *We want what we want because the other person has it. Mimetic rivalry escalates until a scapegoat is found.*

When Alice came back down, Sena served the coffee and after we had drunk it we turned our cups over on their saucers, thinking, as we had been instructed, of a wish.

Let Tom and I make it. I wish for Tom and me to make it.

Sena picked up my cup and put it to the side. I stared at the coffee semicircle left in my saucer and watched it start to turn in on itself.

I am five, sitting cross-legged in my row on the scuffed parquet floor. It is school assembly and some older kids are up at the front with the headmaster, showing off their work. Paper-plate masks with gum and tissue paper shapes stuck on to make faces. The headmaster is holding up one of the masks so we can all see and pointing to parts of it.

'Who knows the name of this shape?'

He points to a nose on one of the masks and calls on someone who says *triangle*.

'What about this one?'

He is pointing to one of the mouths. I don't remember raising my hand, but I remember giving my answer: a semicircle. He is clapping and nodding. I am promised a prize once we return to our classrooms.

The prize is a box of fruit pastels. Not a packet, but a whole box. The prize is here in the classroom, but there is also some confusion. I can see the box – it is mostly green, with a picture of sparkling sweets on the front – and Sinead and I are in the corridor with another teacher. I'm not sure that I am saying anything; I am watching my prize and waiting. This other teacher, the one who has been sent to deliver my prize, looks down at us.

'Now which one of you was it that answered the question in assembly?'

As I raise my hand, Sinead does the same. Then we both say *me* at the same time.

'Well, it can't have been both of you. Which one of you was it?'

Sinead speaks again. 'It was me.'

With another practised flick of her wrist, Sena turned Alice's cup the right way up. On her saucer was a perfect black circle. Alice took a ginger snap from the open packet on the table.

'Is that good?'

Sena shook her head. 'This is the problem with not using the right cups. A perfect circle should be incredibly rare. A perfect, sealed circle means that the answer to your question is yes: whatever it was that you wished for, it will come true.'

Alice laughed. 'I very much doubt it.'

'Next time I go home I will bring back a proper set of Turkish coffee cups. So. Now I will read the grinds.'

She picked up my cup and stared for a long time at its contents.

The point wasn't pushed. We were strange little girls and nobody was quite sure what to do with us. The teacher gave us both the box of sweets and at playtime we distributed them between us as was appropriate: yellows and oranges for her, blacks and reds for me, greens equally divided.

'I see many, many things here,' Sena said, looking into my cup. 'This shape here?' She pointed. 'It makes me think of the port of Alexandria. It's the shape of the causeway that leads to Pharos Island and the old fort.'

There was something about Alexandria on the news the other day. Was it in Egypt? Something awful –

'And there are lots of birds, but mostly their wings seem to have been clipped. You see here?' She pointed to a pyramid of small brown marks on the side of the cup. 'The birds are piling up, but they cannot fly.' She pointed out a section of brown marks further round. 'Here there are two figures – can you see? – they are facing each other but also facing away. It is as if they are both wearing masks on the backs of their heads. They are both looking at one another and also not. And see here – there is another figure. See the cross-like shape? It is as if the figure is being crucified. There, see the crown of thorns on her head?'

The brown and white surface unfurled before me like a painting, figures emerging from smudges. A battery-hen egg factory. The muffled beat of pinned wings straining to flap, beakless birds, their gnarled clawed feet treading on the faces of the beakless birds below. In the brown and white marks, the birds repeated their movements over and over, a stinking squawking roar of thwarted instinct.

'That's it, I think. That's all I see at the moment. Does it mean anything to you?'

I blinked and looked up at Sena. Her expression said take-it-or-leave-it. I looked over at Alice; hers was one of concern. I made myself laugh.

'Plenty to think about there!'

The other important thing about mimesis is that it is forbidden. The day I read that in the library was the last day I spent there. It was coming to the end of that strange summer, and not long after I moved in with Alice, met Chloe and I somehow put it all out of my mind. The words were in a turquoise book that was almost completely indecipherable, but as I scanned through it I found sentences seemed to circle in on themselves, full of words like *terror* and *magic* and *otherness*. I didn't understand what the book was about or even its title – *Dialectic of Enlightenment* by Max Horkheimer and Theodor W. Adorno –

but I was finding things I recognised. And then there was this: *uncontrolled mimesis was outlawed. Certain gestures and forms of behaviour . . . shameful residues . . . the forbidden. Gestures of touching, nestling, soothing, coaxing . . . mimesis unto death.* The mimetic faculty, I suddenly knew, was what they were testing for in the test they'd made Sinead do. I also knew that these evenings in the darkness with the books were only taking me further in the wrong direction. I needed to be sane. I needed to stop thinking, stop reading and be sane. That night, on the way to the bus stop, I threw my notebook in a bin.

The problem was, after that coffee-ground reading, mimesis was now all I could think about. The way Alice always had a cloth, tissue or wet wipe in her hand. The way she leant over and wiped egg and yogurt from Rose's mouth, then swiped the tabletop, gathering the crumbs into her palm. She wiped spit, and picked up half-chewed food from T-shirts and stuffed toys. Sometimes her findings went into the bin, but more often than not they were moved absent-mindedly into her pocket or onto the nearest empty surface, the top of a chest of drawers or a counter, as she turned to attend to one of the children.

Mimesis was a kind of magic, a *sympathetic magic*, one that decreed that things which have touched will continue to act on one other even at a distance, even after the physical contact has been severed: an unfamiliar hair in your soup; another's fingerprints smeared across a touch screen; all accidental raw material for making it so.

And something about soap. I'd written something about soap in that notebook. *Contagion. The laws of similarity.*

Soap being anti-mimetic. All those strange dark words. I can't get them out of my mind.

Sinead holding onto my arm. Can a spell be cast unwittingly? If there is a wishing or a strong enough feeling, near enough to the correct ingredients, can it be made so? Names or thrice-repeated desires expressed in a nail bar or a hairdressers; the desire for revenge among the correct amount of semen and spit.

Me! Jinx! Whoever shouts *Jinx* last must stay silent until the winner proclaims their full name. Unless the name is said, the curse remains unlifted. Sinead's fingers on my arm. For years, it was only at sacraments – christenings, communions, Christmases and cousins' weddings – that we would ever touch. At school in RE, Sister Bridget used to tell us how all the sacraments contain manifestations of the sacred; all I know is that, at such dos people want to take pictures. With all the *Move in a bit closer, whose phone is this? How does the timer work? Say cheese!* bodies get mixed up and suddenly, with all the shifting and the pushing and the swishing of dresses, arms can end up around waists and over shoulders and I can feel her in there, underneath her skin.

C ooking that first night at Alice's, as the dark evening had spread along the lawn, I looked down at that butternut squash, split open on the wooden chopping board. The strange shock of its flat, peach flesh, wrong and somehow blind, simultaneously too empty and too full.

My first thought had been of the new iPhone. Apple had removed the headphone port and the reason they had given for this was *courage – the courage to move on and do something new that betters us all.* There was also a video that had appeared on YouTube around the time of the phone's release. Styled like a home DIY tutorial, the phone was put into a metal vice while an authoritative voice-over promised to explain how to reveal the hidden socket. A hole was then drilled into the bottom of the phone. Once this was done, the phone was removed from the vice, headphones were plugged in and music played. Judging from the angry comments below, this advice was actually followed by quite a few phone owners.

As well as the espresso machine, Wren liked to watch *Paw Patrol* and play with her wooden train track. The track was laid out on the floorboards in the sitting room. I knelt down inside the broken figure-of-eight while she attached a carriage to the front engine. There were Lego buildings at intervals around the track and some kind of space ship near one of the tunnels.

'This one goes around there.'

'Okay.'

'And then through here.'

'Okay.'

'But you have to make yours go that way.'

'Right.' I position my train as instructed.

'You go through the tunnel and round there and I come this way.' She shows me how it's going to work.

'Then what happens?'

'Then we crash!'

Old incantations:

Wait. Stop the game.

Let's pretend that you didn't do that and I did this.

No, let's pretend I said this, then you said that, then –

No, let's pretend that you did this and then I did that –

Then I say –

No, then you say –

Common among the various theories on what makes a game a game are these factors: the formal limits of a restricted code and a controllable shape, a quantifiable notion of success, a variable outcome and a known end point. Game designers offer this further elaboration: toys + goals = puzzles; puzzles + competitor = competition; competition + conflict = game.

'Oh, and the airplane. Wasn't it lovely, wasn't it?'

'Wasn't it? Wasn't it lovely, wasn't it?'

When we were nine years old, our great-aunts came to visit from Ireland. They were also identical twins.

'Wasn't it? It was just lovely, wasn't it?'

'Oh, it was. Just lovely.'

They brought us two small green teddy bears, a shamrock sewn on to each of their stomachs. We ran upstairs to decide who would get which. It was immediately clear that one was good and one was evil. Coins were tossed, deals made and names given: Lucky was the good one – we would take it in turns to have him – and Shady was the evil one. I lost the toss so I had to take Shady down to the garage and shove it behind the big chest freezer.

Wren's mastery of the iPad was impressive, her swipe measured and her touch precise. There was, however, something unnerving about the way the episode of *Paw Patrol* misinformed her about matter. The CGI fireman dog and his various pals were horribly weightless, speeding about while seeming to make no contact with the ladder they climbed, the truck they drove, or each other. This, added to the unconvincing lip-sync, was making me nauseous. When Wren got bored and wandered off to find her mum, I paused the cartoon and was left alone, kneeling in silence in the ring of track.

I heard Wren in the kitchen requesting hot tea and I heard Alice murmuring back as she put away crockery. Arranged around me in the circle were a wet wipe, two odd socks and a half-eaten banana. I closed my eyes as Richard called out from the floor above:

'Wren! Go and wash your hands for supper.' There was a pause before he shouted again: 'And use soap!'

S itting by the river all those years ago. In the circle of doubled bridge was a doubled swan. It had a head at the bottom as well as the top, like a tarot card deity. I looked over at Chloe to see if she'd seen it.

'Do you ever feel like there is a portal or something near you? And if you knew how, you could just slip through it?'

'Slip through it to where?'

'You slip through and suddenly you are someone else.'

'I'm pretty sure I don't believe in portals. Lack of empirical evidence and all that.'

The doubled swan bent its neck and dipped its beak into

the water. A sign is a sign is a sign. That's the thing about the *mise en abyme*. I put a hand on either side of Chloe's face and kissed her mouth. It just keeps going.

Make a lather out of the salt of a fatty acid as a boundary between the self and the other. A thin layer of triglycerides to prevent assimilating, to prevent merging, to prevent yielding or any sliding back. Lather to ward off the longing, to protect yourself from return. Lather and seek out smooth, fully sealed edges.

I heard recently that they had to attach anti-suicide nets around the walls of China's Foxconn factory where iPhones get made. And surely each iPhone or iPad, each gadget, portless or not, still carries microscopic but material traces of spit, skin and hair? Supply chain sympathetic magic tangling us up in the wishes of those we never see.

'You know when I was cooking that squash curry?'
    Wren was playing on the lawn beside the buggy and Alice and I were standing nearby, drinking tea. Alice called out – 'Wren, remember to be careful of your sister!' – then motioned for me to continue.
    'When I first cut the squash open, I thought they had found a way to make them completely seedless.'
    'Seedless?'
    'Actually, I just hadn't cut down far enough, but for a minute I thought that they had found a way to make the whole thing flesh - you know, to somehow do away with the seed bit. Like a coreless apple or something.'

'Can you get a coreless apple?'

'No – I don't think so.'

Alice looked over at Wren, checking she wasn't making a move on her sister. She turned back to me. 'Right. So you thought it didn't have seeds but really it did?'

'Yeah. But it made me think. What is it with all these sealed-up devices? What is it with getting rid of all the holes?'

'Wren!' Alice took a step towards her daughter. 'Remember she's your sister and you love her!' She looked back towards me as she walked away. 'Sorry! I know, right? A new gadget comes out every day. Richard is such a sucker for all of that.'

As Alice walked towards her, I watched Wren perform what she imagined her mother thought love looked like: she reached for her sister and patted her on the head. Alice laughed. 'That's good. That's nice. Good girl.' She turned back to me again and smiled.

That was when I suddenly remembered what it was about Alexandria that made the news. Nine Somalians, migrants moving through Egypt to try to reach Europe, had been found dead on the beach. Two of the nine were babies and a third was their mother. All of their torsos had been cut open and crudely stitched back together. Vital organs were missing, believed to have been sold.

Alice was next to me again. She slipped her arm through mine. 'That curry was great, by the way. What was that weird yellow stuff you said you put in it?'

On the drive home from camping in the Hidden Valley, Tom and I stop at an old village pub. He goes to the bar and I sit at a small, round table in the corner, near a shelf of tourist leaflets. The table is very wobbly. The kind of thing that would impress my dad is if with no fuss at all, you picked up a beer mat, folded it, slid it under the correct leg, then sat back up and continued drinking your pint. The mat exactly the right thickness and the wobble totally gone. But if it didn't work first time, that'd be worse than even trying and if you were too nonchalant, he might hate you for having done it when he hadn't.

After I watched that Alistair Cooke documentary, I looked up how autumn leaves got their colours. When the soil is poor, branches hold on to their leaves for as long as they can, so that as much goodness as possible can be absorbed back into the tree. As nutrients and chlorophyll are absorbed, the green pigment fades and the other colours – the yellows and the oranges – become visible.

The red pigment, however, has a plan all of its own. The red comes from a chemical called anthocyanin and when the red leaves fall to the ground they cause a process known as *allelopathy* – *allelo* means to be in a reciprocal relationship and *pathy* means suffering. Once on the ground, the anthocyanin leaches out into the soil around the tree's base and acts as a growth inhibitor, making sure that only its own seedlings are able to survive there.

There are a few people already ordering drinks. I watch Tom lean on the bar. Him saying, *I don't know what else to do*. There had been a note in his voice that I'd not heard before. I flick through the leaflets. What am I supposed to do about something I don't even understand myself? A pile for Glencoe Visitor Centre and sea kayaking; a pile for a steam train at Fort William; a lone one for a nearby Indian curry house. There is also a dog-eared *Rough Guide to the Scottish Highlands and Islands* with the words DO NOT STEAL written across the front in black marker. I open it at random. The Isle of Inchkeith. A ferry time-table. A picture of some kind of old military fort.

There is a saying about love being a verb, an action, rather than a feeling. But what if love is a memory? What if whoever you decide to love, *how*ever you decide to love, all your *verbing* – the real thing only feels like the real thing because you recognise it? What three words can I use to describe how I feel when Tom and I begin to have sex? No words come when I try to think about it. We start and then, as things develop, as he moves on top of me or I move on top of him, as the possibility gets closer and closer to becoming a reality, I stop. I push him away, roll off him or out from under him. *What's wrong?* he asks.

What three words mark this spot? These days, he doesn't even ask what's wrong anymore. He just sighs and turns over or gets up and puts his T-shirt back on. I am watching it happening, watching our ending beginning.

Tom is speaking to the woman behind the bar. Laughing his lovely laugh. I don't want to start thinking about this. I just want us to have a nice time. For him to laugh and forget how difficult I am. I return my focus to the page: Inchkeith. In the Firth of Forth. Volcanic rock. Lowest average annual rainfall in Scotland. Was this the island we'd seen when we sat on Portobello beach last year?

I read: *The Island is said to be a caol ait – a Celtic phrase for thin place.* Caol ait. A thin place. *A place where the boundary between heaven and earth, or past and present, is particularly thin.*

All the times when someone has come up to me in the street grinning or shouting hello. Sometimes this stranger hugs me. That horrible moment of slippage. As I awkwardly feign a response to the sudden hug, I slip into that place, that place where I am unseen and trapped at the same time. Dad playing with me, tickling me, there with me, and then suddenly calling me by her name. That feeling of free-fall, that disappearing; the world you thought you knew dissolving into lies.

Sinead and I swapped classes once at school and nobody noticed. We were twelve. I went to her class and she went to mine. In the toilets, during lunch, we put our hair up into the same kind of ponytail and reminded each other to keep our lips over our teeth so that the brace and the bracelessness wouldn't show. When the bell rang, I walked up a different set of stairs and sat at a different desk.

To start with it was fun, the thrill of being a spy in a different class, but then there was the moment when I started to panic. What if no one ever noticed? I'd be stuck here, inside a body that wasn't mine, forever. I'd be looking out of the eye holes of this face but no one would know I was in here. The feeling got so bad I had to tell Sinead's teacher I was going to be sick. I went to my real classroom and looked in through the glass panel in the door. I could see her. She was laughing with Charlotte who sat at the desk beside me. Charlotte never laughed with me. I stood watching her through the glass. It was like she was somehow *realer* than I was –

I stretch my arms up over my head. Stretch and move on. I look back down at the book and scan the section on the island's history. *An experiment on the origins of mankind's God-given language was conducted in 1493 by King James IV.* Interesting. *The king sent a mute woman and two newborn babies to live on the island to find out . . . some historical sources record the babies as being twins.* Christ.

The mute and the babies are banished to the island and after seven years the king visits. Some records say that the twins' only means of communication was a seagull-like caw or a goat-like bleat; others say that they became fluent in Hebrew, or drowned, or that the experiment was never really carried out. I close the book and stare at the picture of misted green peaks underneath the marker pen message. What I need is to *do* something. Less thinking, more action. I need to *do* something before –

A lake, surrounded by a mountain range and reflecting the pure blue of the sky. In the corner of the cover is a little white logo. I lift the book closer to see it. A running figure circled by the words *Make the Most of Your Time On Earth*. I need to *do* something, change something –

'She says there's a great fish and chip shop a bit further along the main road.'

Tom puts a pint in front of me and sits down. I take a sip.

'I've decided to go and help out at the camp in Calais.'

B efore I have a chance to change my mind I've booked a week off work, a ferry from Dover to Calais, and I'm on the coach, my face staring back at me in every tunnel.

The ferry's Quiet Room is opposite the cafeteria and has been insulated somehow, cutting out the rumbling of the engine. I'm the only one in here, sitting beside a large plastic yukka plant and a nailed-down table. I read some advice on the No Borders website: *Radical solidarity means working together as equals while charity involves the implicit division between the givers and recipients of aid. It may feel like you are better 'doing something' rather than nothing at all but –* The rocking of the boat is starting to make me feel sick. I look out of the large rounded window; there is nothing but blueness, a flat horizon, the above slightly paler than the below.

Later, in the cafeteria area, I watch a TV screen showing CCTV footage of stacked pet crates accompanied by a pop muzak soundtrack. It's a live stream for people who want to watch their pets in the ferry's Pet Hotel. In grey boxes, dogs are sleeping or barking, and cats are scratching or looking out between the bars. Every five seconds the frame switches to show another section of cages.

T he youth hostel that I have booked is full of out-of-town gendarmes employed to patrol the camp. When we sit for breakfast at the long tables normally used for school or foreign exchange groups, some of them are already in their police uniforms. They queue with their trays to get bread and jam and to fill their mugs with coffee. We pass the water jug along to one another and, after I have been there a few days, we begin to nod and smile: *Bonjour, Bonjour.*

The camp warehouse is in an industrial estate and teeming with volunteers. I stand in the makeshift kitchen beside a pile of liability waiver forms, hoping to become useful. Around me, people in fluorescent hi-vis vests stack tins, fold T-shirts and tie pairs of shoes together by their laces. A man from Bath tells me that they are creating starter packs: a sleeping bag, a tent, a blanket and a pair of shoes for each arrival. Other people are making hot drinks or washing up.

I join a queue, put a teabag in a mug and hold it under a metal urn full of coffee.

I am tipping my mistake into a slops bucket under the table when a short-haired woman, wearing batik and battered suede, pushes her way through.

'God, it's so *busy*. Who *are* all these people?' She stops to speak to someone in hi-vis, then claps her hands. 'Okay, everybody. Outside.'

We all move into the yard, where sacks of rice are being hauled into shopping trolleys, crates of tinned tomatoes and chickpeas unloaded from the backs of vans.

'Make a circle! A big, big circle!'

I slot in beside a girl with dyed red hair and a woman wearing an old *Make Poverty History* T-shirt. I remember a project Tom told me about, volunteers who went out to help build a school somewhere in Peru. They spent all their days working on the new structure, then at night, when they were asleep, the men from the town silently dismantled it. Secretly, they took the volunteers' work

106

down piece by piece, replacing it with foundations fit for use and properly applied mortar.

'That's right, nice and big! Okay, now let's warm ourselves up with some nice big star jumps!'

My blue surgical gloves slip as I put them into the most disgusting bit I can find. A pile of rotting rice, onion skin and eggshells. I have been allocated a job as a camp litter picker. I drop the mush into a black binbag and scoop up some more. Mostly there is mud. And in it, shabby tents, gaffer-taped huts and portaloos. Men with scarves over their faces are walking slowly, their heads down, wearing only T-shirts despite the rain. The tented areas are quite clean, but as soon as you move away there are piles of rubbish and torn plastic bags. Among the rotting food are full tins of beans or fruit, cans that are rusted on top and misshapen by failed attempts to get inside without a tin opener. As well as old food and litter there are trails of clothes: frozen scarves and twisted jumpers, socks origamied hard into the soil.

Seagulls are beaking at overflowing binbags and everybody is sockless. I scoop up the rubbish and try to make myself meet the eyes of two stony-faced men. I am feeling their stare, full of things I will never know, full of contempt for my privilege – so it shocks me when they wave, shouting thank you and welcome, their faces splitting with smiles.

There are 10,000 people at the camp when I visit. I serve chai tea to some of them from an enormous metal pot. One man comes to stand next to it, putting a palm on either of its hot sides and smiling. I smile back and he stays there silently for a long time, other men pushing past him to hand me their plastic beakers or jars. Some men fill their cups nearly half full with sugar first, some say, Good morning, how are you today, I am fine. There are a few adolescent boys, two in particular, who just say, Full. No matter how full I make their jars they motion for me to fill them up further, refusing to take them until I have added one more drop. Towards the end of the afternoon a man in a short-sleeved shirt and glasses comes to get his tea.

'You are English?'

I tell him that I am, but that I live in Scotland. I always say this, using Glasgow like a shield. He waves away the difference with his hand.

'You must contact your government. Speak to your Member of Parliament. It is you, the British, who have caused such disruption in the world. With your empire and your map-making and your line-drawing. We flee now from problems you have made. You must make your government act. Make them offer more asylum. I was a lecturer at the university in Damascus. I taught politics. I know about international relations.'

I tell him he is right and fill up his plastic beaker. Another man hands me a cup and I fill that too. I watch the lecturer take his tea over to the table with the sugar. He adds two spoonfuls and stirs, then pushes his glasses up on his nose, blows and takes a sip.

The next day I offer my services in the kitchen and get to ladle out grout-like porridge at breakfast.

'Porridge?'

Some men shake their heads, they want tea and biscuits; others hold out their bowls.

Libby is another volunteer in the kitchen. She is twenty-two, from Clapham and wearing ethnic-print harem trousers and a multicoloured jumper. Hettie is around the same age and from Stroud. She has just finished studying at a circus school in Bristol and has a set of little glittery stickers that she sticks on some of the men's faces. Mette is from Iraq and has been living in the camp for four days; he comes over to the table where we are chopping.

'I am chef. I show you.' He takes the onion from Hettie. 'One two. One two three. Look.' He slices another. 'One two. One two three. You see? Like that. Give me ten.'

The washing-up station is four plastic buckets. The first is very hot and soapy, the second very hot and less soapy, the third is for rinsing and the fourth has a towel at the bottom for drying. Dhal-smeared plastic is piling up. Some men bring their plates over when they are done; others leave them on the tables or on the floor. Libby is scraping, Florence – a retired maths teacher – is clearing the tables and I am drying plastic children's cutlery.

After lunch, ten or fifteen men stay, standing at the back of the eating area and trying to connect their phones to the fluctuating Wi-Fi. A man called Abdel has joined me at the washing-up station. He asks how long I have been here.

'It's my fourth day. What about you?'

'Six months.'

'How are you doing?'

'My friend is also from Sudan. He has been here for a

year. Every night, we will try until we make it to the UK.'

I dry a plate with a wet towel. 'Every night?'

'Yes. There is only one chance.'

'Only one chance?'

'Life. Life is only one chance. '

Hettie leans over to the mini-speaker resting on a crate of carrots and turns up Manu Chao. Libby begins rocking her hips and shoulders.

'Compulsory dancing at the washing-up station!'

The row of men at the back of the tent look up as the two girls begin to shimmy, passing their crockery to the beat.

I hear there is another camp down the road from this main one. Dunkirk is much worse, people say. John, a volunteer driver who'd been working at the warehouse for six months, is about to make a delivery there.

'Can I help?'

'Sure.'

I start to pass him boxes from the trolley, so he can load them into the back of the van. The taped-up boxes have SHOES and JUMPERS written on their sides. Dunkirk. We shall fight on the beaches. Little boats making their heroic journeys across the channel. A box with HATS on the side. When the van is packed, I wheel the trolley over to the other side of the yard, then run back over.

'Can I come with you?'

'It's a whole different story at Dunkirk. No one wants to do the distribution drop there.'

He walks around to the driver's seat and gets in. I open

the passenger door and climb in beside him. He looks at me, shrugs and starts the engine.

Volunteers need a permit to enter the Dunkirk camp. The road approaching it and the entrance are heavily policed. Clearly they weren't going to let what happened in the Jungle happen here: no art classes, no theatre productions and no do-gooders. Wooden structures and shipping containers are being set up at the far end of a field. The gendarmes search the van before we are allowed to enter – no tents, sleeping bags or blankets are allowed in. As we drive through the gate, I see a line of men, maybe fifty or more, already waiting. As we park up and get out, they close in on the van. John asks them to move back so he can open the rear doors and unload the goods. Soon, he is motioning with his hands and shouting:

'Get back. *Revenir!*'

The men are pushing and jostling to remain at the front of the crowd while reluctantly taking very small steps backwards. I stand to the side of the van ready to start unpacking the boxes. John is unlocking the rear door, still shouting for everyone to get back. As he begins to open it the men crowd in again so there is no room for it to swing out. He uses the right-hand door to force the crowd back, then does the same on the other side.

'Make a line! *Tracer une ligne!*'

He gestures to indicate he wants the men to form a queue. There is some shuffling sideways and some shouting and then a man wearing a woollen hat shoves John out of the way and climbs into the van himself. He tears open a box, pulls out a tied-together pair of trainers and hangs them over his shoulder. He begins throwing shoes out into the crowd. One man catches a pair of boots and begins to unlace them, pushing his mud-caked bare feet inside. Another man jumps into the van and the next thing I know, John is down in the mud. Boots are flying and John is trying to get up.

'Get out of the van! Make a queue and I will –'

I start moving towards John but there is a scuffle over another pair of boots and I too find myself on my knees in the mud. A bearded older man, holding a wellington boot, offers me his hand and pulls me up. Something moves through his eyes, as if he is about to say something, then suddenly he dives down between the legs of a man beside us, returning with the other welly. I see two men facing one another, each holding one new-looking walking boot, the knotted laces taut between them. They are slowly moving in towards one another, their eyes locked. One has a blanket around his shoulders and his face is hard, his eyes fierce. John is on his feet and back in the van, pulling men away from the boxes and forcing them out. The man holding the boot closest to me suddenly lets go and walks quickly away, sandalled feet tramping across the boggy ground. The man with the blanket puts the pair of boots underneath it and wraps it more tightly around himself.

'MAKE A LINE OR WE WILL DRIVE AWAY.'

John is alone in the back of the van now, screaming out instructions. The men who have already acquired shoes are walking away, or hopping, putting their new shoes on as they go. The men who are left slowly shuffle into something like a queue. John motions for me to stand at the front and tells me to only give a pair of shoes to those who do not already have adequate footwear. He hands me a pair of wellies. The man at the front of the line is wearing a baseball cap with a Union Jack on it. I look down at his feet. He is wearing torn trainers. Are they adequate? Compared to what? My eyes meet his. His expression is sardonic.

'You give me the boots or no?'

I hand him the wellies.

It was in the van, driving back to the warehouse, that John told me about Raheemullah Oryakhel. A fourteen-year-old boy, run over by a truck on the ring road around the port. He and a friend had been on top of a container that was attached to a lorry. They had made a hole in the roof and were climbing inside but Raheemullah slipped when the driver swerved to shake them off. His friend reported that the container was full of office chairs. John had spoken to a few of the men who were near the ring road at the time and they told him that before the truck coming the other way had hit Raheemullah, it had sped up. He drove fast on purpose, one of them said. The lorry drivers hate us. They think we should all just disappear.

That night, I join some of the volunteers at a bar in town.

'It's like two worlds that have been parallel to each other are now able to meet – the free-party world and the refugee world.'

The man talking has a goatee and earrings. 'Both are outside of mainstream society, but it's like both have found a way, in the Jungle, to make something, to build something.'

'*Parallel?*' I say it more sharply than I mean to.

'Like running alongside each other?'

'Yeah. I know what parallel means.'

He looks confused, then patient. 'The free-party people, the festival people – they are the only ones who are stepping up to help.'

Someone else joins in. 'It's like a global festival. A festival for all those that reject capitalism, those that reject racism –'

I drain my beer and slide away down the bar to order another. I find myself next to an older man. He turns around.

'You are one of the volunteers?'

He has a French accent. I nod.

'A do-gooder,' he says.

I shrug.

'Well, let me tell you, *bonne âme*, it's the truck drivers for whom I feel sorry. They take a fine of 2,000 euros for finding a migrant in their truck. And what does a *putain* trucker earn?

I down another beer, then walk back to the hostel. My mind is full. The dhal smell in the kitchen, the suds on plastic plates. Those oblivious dancing girls. Me, jumping into the van, desperate to go see Dunkirk. It's dark and I'm walking past the tall blocks of flats that circle the town centre. The men at the back of the tent with their unreadable eyes. But worse, that man with readable eyes. Me, holding those wellies, deciding whether or not to give them to him. And that boy. That van speeding up, the driver needing to make him disappear. I realise I'm crying. That man's look as I stood with the wellies. It was how Sinead had looked at me, sitting on the hospital bed.

She had come back from doing the test and Mum and Dad had gone out to talk to the doctor.

'Crazy test! Crazy questions!'

As she started to list the questions again, I could already feel the *No* growing.

'So I ticked B. I mean, because, obviously! It's like a test to see if you're human!'

It took her a while to notice. 'What are you doing? Are you listening?'

That silent sliding door.

'Look,' I heard myself say. 'You should try and stay calm.'

Her laugh was wide and open. 'What?'

'And if, you know, you're taking drugs, you should stop.'

Her laugh was incredulous now. 'What the fuck are you doing?' I stood and watched the fear rise in her eyes. She stood up in her paper robe. 'What the fuck are you doing?'

She could see the door; she could see it sliding shut and she could see which side she was being left on. 'Stop it! Stop staring at me like that!'

'Seriously. You should really try and stay calm.'

Her mouth didn't know what to do with itself. Her eyes were widening. Bewilderment, confusion. Realisation. Betrayal. Fury. 'Don't you fucking dare. Don't you fucking –'

'Look.' My new voice. 'Why don't we just wait and see what your test scores say. I'm sure it'll all be fine.'

She was red-faced now, her mouth a snarl. It was like I'd never seen her before, and now, from so far away, I could. Rather than feeling with her, I could watch her. And as I watched her, I felt something glowing within me: I felt bigger, stronger. Pity, I realised, this was how pity felt. Suddenly her face shifted. The fear lifted for a fraction of a second and her eyes met mine. This was the same bitter look that the man queuing for his wellies had given me. A look that said, *I see you. I see what is happening here.* Then she started to cry.

My grandmother used to say I'd be careful pulling that face; when the wind changes you'll be stuck. But we already knew about moments of wind and change. We already knew how with a sudden word or a name, everything that had been swapping and sliding freely between us could change – that sudden sealing, and how whatever you grabbed in that moment became who you were. It was like musical chairs when the music stopped, but with everything, instead of just chairs.

A t breakfast, a primary school teacher helping at the camp during half-term tells me that a Calais council official has just announced that all occupants of the camp are due to be bussed to reception centres elsewhere in a week. The camp is to be dismantled. *There is a balance to be struck,* the official had argued, *between meeting basic humanitarian needs and not attracting more migrants.*

In the afternoon, I go to the big white school tent to help with English conversation class. In broken English, Bashir tells me that his family were farmers in Afghanistan. Open on his lap is a Cambridge Advanced English textbook. He asks if I will help explain, and points to the word *Conscientious*.

'It's like careful,' I say. 'Like wanting everything to be just right; like studying very hard.'

I do a mime of wearing spectacles and looking at a book. He nods. 'Okay. Okay.'

I feel good. This is good. I'm helping. He points to the word *During*. I think for a while. 'That's a difficult one. It's like time. During this time, we are talking; during dinner time we are eating; during the night we are sleeping.' He shakes his head and waits for more. I try again: '*During* is the period of time in which something is happening. It's a section of time.'

He shakes his head and points to *Opposite*. I mime shivering and then basking in the sun. 'Cold is the opposite of hot. Or good and bad.' I mime telling someone off and then smiling. 'Good is the opposite of bad.'

He is smiling. 'Yes, yes, very good. Good and bad. Opposite.'

I suddenly notice that other volunteers around us are using whiteboards and playing language-learning games. I don't have anything. What the fuck am I doing here?

'Look. Listen. If you want to go and learn with someone else – I mean . . .'

'You need to go?'

'No. No, I don't need to go. But maybe it will be better for you if . . .'

He looks confused. Then he nods. 'I see. You have no –' He stops to think. 'You have no . . .' He taps the shoulder of a man in the next group. 'My friend. How do you say *Sabor?*'

The man turns around. '*Sabor? Sabor* is patience.'

The light is fading as I pass restaurants and boulangeries and walk over the bridge again. Seagulls are calling out in the pale light and in the distance I can see the ferry terminal. A family, English-looking, are walking along the road in bright holiday clothes, the little boy licking an ice cream. I've read that some Eastern European truckers are paid so little they can't even afford accommodation en route – they have to live in their trucks for weeks on end. I think of my dad's dad, coming over from Ireland and driving a Michelin truck for thirty years. Long journeys delivering tyres, watching the trails of red and white lights, then going back home to his family, to his vegetables. He used to take my dad or his brothers with him sometimes, stopping in a lay-by to eat cheese sandwiches and a packet of crisps. My phone rings. It's Tom.

'How's it going?'

'It's strange.'

'I bet.'

'Not just the place itself, or the conditions. I mean the volunteers. The whole set-up.'

'How d'you mean?'

'I can't put my finger on it. There's this festival vibe – it feels so wrong – like some kind of theme park of awfulness – but – I don't know. How are you?'

Tom tells me he misses me, that he's in the pub with work people, that he just came out to say a quick hello, to check I was doing okay. 'It's great you're there, that you're helping –'

'Is it? Am I? Anyway. Thanks for ringing. I'll see you in a few days.'

I spend my last day in the women and children's area. It is a large wooden structure covered in tarpaulin, softly lit and smelling of joss sticks. The women are sitting in small groups and a couple of young children are spinning around and falling dizzily onto cushions. Saturday is Beauty Day; there is nail painting and behind a draped net curtain, back massages.

There is a knock at the door. I pull the makeshift bolt back and open it a crack. The person guarding the door on the outside says: 'Some more visitors.'

Two smiling, headscarfed women step in. One hugs a volunteer with a notebook and adds her name to the list for eyebrow threading. I shut the door and re-bolt it. From the far end of the room someone calls out: 'Can anyone do French plaits?'

The volunteer next to me says that she can.

'Will you be okay being bouncer on your own?'

I say I'll be fine and she laughs, delighted. 'At last! I have a useful skill!'

A woman is putting on her shoes and getting ready to leave. She is wearing men's Caterpillar boots without socks. When she gets to the door she holds out her glittery blue nails for me to see.

'Look!'

'What a great colour!'

As she calls out behind her to the room – 'Thank you, thank you!' – her toddler son takes hold of her hand and steps into his wellies. She pulls up his hood.

'Thank the ladies.'

'Thank you!' he says with a big smile. 'Thank you,

119

thank you, fuck you.'

'No, no. Just *thank you*.' She looks at me, embarrassed. 'He means thank you. I tell it to him.'

He looks at me, hard eyed, and spits the words out again: 'Fuck you.'

She crouches down beside him and takes his hands. 'No, no. To the ladies we say *thank you*. *Fuck you* is just for the police.'

On the ferry back, I sit in the Quiet Room again. After a while, tiny white spikes appear, way off in the rocking blue. A host of offshore wind turbines lined up in rows, some slowly turning, others not. I think about Bashir. He had told me that he spent his mornings in the school and in the afternoon he studied in his tent. Each night, after eating, he went to the tunnel to try and break into a truck. When the English session had ended, he had shaken my hand. *Sabor* is important, he said. Especially for people living in the Jungle. With *sabor* I will become very good at English, will come to England and will have a good life.

He had taken a mug of tea from me at dinner later that evening.

'Good evening.' He smiled. 'You are here tomorrow too?'

'No. I go home tonight.'

'Tonight!' In his hand he held a Weetabix and two rich tea biscuits. 'And have you enjoyed your holiday in the Jungle?'

It is dark by the time the coach pulls in for a rest stop at Gretna Green motorway services. Birds are flocking overhead, more and more arriving, their calls getting louder. I eat a Scotch egg and watch them swoop and meet, circling the car park. Flocking birds were something Sinead and I used to love. Maybe it was the way that each one seemed to already know what the others were thinking. Back on the motorway, there is a winding row of white lights up ahead, and in the blackness on either side of the road I can just make out the curve of the hills.

Tom stirs the pasta sauce as the radio reports on the upcoming Calais camp clearance.

'Are you still glad you went?'

'Who knows? I keep thinking about how I would respond if I was in the situation they are in, if I was that desperate.'

Tom mixes the sauce into the spaghetti. 'Yeah.'

'I mean, I'd be all right, right? I'd be good?'

'What do you mean?'

'I'd – sometimes I worry that I'd –' I falter as he starts dishing the pasta out into bowls.

'Stop comparing.'

'What? With the men at the camp?'

'What? No. The bowls.'

'I'm not.' He looks at me. I shrug. 'Except that you *have* got more mushrooms than me.'

As I walk to the night shelter, the street lights are glowing against the purpling sky. Car headlights

121

spread wetly on the tarmac. Starlings wheel about together overhead. I now know that murmuration works because all the birds follow a few sensible rules: not too close, not too fast, not too slow. An instinctual algorithm that produces the illusion of choreography and communication. I also now know that during the migratory season, caged birds put on weight and become nocturnal. They store up fat to prepare for flights they are never going to make, then they hop and flutter around in their cages at night, whirring their wings as if they are on their way.

In the limbo of the TV room, we make small talk and joke about our failures to communicate. Gestures are large and crucial, men acting and pulling funny faces to make themselves understood. We watch blockbuster films and communicate via the celebs, the common language of Brad Pitt, Julia Roberts and Bruce Willis. Dinner time is tense, especially if there is meat. Some of the men wander the halls and hang around in the driveway, waiting to see what is left over after the others have eaten, wanting to avoid any trouble.

I wonder again how many of the men at the night shelter came through the Calais camp. Volunteers are advised not to ask the men for their stories. All of them are ILL (Illegal) or ILL CLN (Illegal Clandestine). Most are classed as NRPF (No Recourse to Public Funds) and ARE (Appeal Rights Exhausted). They have all had their IE (Immigration Enforcement) interview and applied for asylum; some have made a SAG (Statement of Additional Grounds) due to being from a PSG (Particular Social Group). Most have had an R (Refusal) letter and requested a RFRL (Reasons for Refusal Letter). Some have never received this. Many of their cases have moved from WIP (Work in Progress) to OOT (Out of Time) and ARE without any official FR (Final Refusal) or RFRL. Many have had encounters with the RCT (Removals and Cessation Team) and spent time in a DET CR (Detention Centre). The men, I am told, are tired of telling their stories, tired of trying to prove how persecuted and desperate they are. Tired of being told that their version of events isn't coherent or convincing enough.

I ring a counselling centre, worrying the whole time that the washing-machine man will ring the doorbell while I'm on the phone. Our machine broke down last week and yesterday, at a local shop selling second-hand white goods, Tom haggled the owner down to fifty quid for a machine plus delivery. The owner was around sixty with a beer gut and that mildly sexist assumption, correct in this case, that Tom would do both the talking and the paying.

A woman's voice answers the phone. 'Hello, how can I help?'

'Hi, I'm calling to see if I can arrange some counselling sessions for my boyfriend and me.'

The counselling centre's receptionist talks me through the sliding scale of fees – two pounds for every thousand the couple earns per annum – and impresses upon me the non-refundable nature of the deposit. The washing-machine man said that he would come between 1 and 5 p.m. and all morning I've been battling a strong desire to clean the house for him.

'That's fine. I'll pay it now.'

As I take my card out of my wallet, I am watching myself through the washing-machine man's eyes: *Sex therapy? Christ. You women.* He is making a face exactly like the one my dad makes.

Sandra sits in front of us holding the clipboards and our forms.

'This is just an assessment session.'

One form contains statements such as *In the last week I have felt in despair* and *In the last week I have felt full of energy and enthusiasm* and options – *often, occasionally* or *rarely* – for us to circle. The other has statements such as *I often really enjoy my partner's sense of humour* and *I would like more sexual intimacy with my partner* and the options – *strongly agree, agree, disagree* or *strongly disagree*.

'It's just a chance for you both to talk about whatever problems you may be having and to see what we, here at the centre, might be able to do to help.'

Tom and I look at each other and he smiles a watery smile. Sandra smiles too. 'When do you think your problems began?'

I motion for Tom to go ahead. He shrugs a little. 'I'd say that things got difficult when we were living in the damp flat. The bed was small and it was cold.'

Tom speaks very formally when he is emotional. Sandra turns to me. 'So that's when your problems started?'

'No. For me, it's always been a problem.'

'I see. Can you explain further?'

'For as long as I can remember. It's always been a problem.'

124

Afterwards, we get a coffee across the road. Tom takes a sip.

'I bet they hear a lot about people's relationships in here.'

'Yeah.'

I put a sugar cube on my spoon and submerge it in my latte, checking its progress until half has dissolved, then putting the spoon and its remaining stickiness onto the saucer. 'I don't want to end up making this all about me and my family, you know? I want it to be about us.'

Tom nods. 'I think that's what she was saying. That all that *is* part of us.'

'I don't want it to be.'

'I know.'

'You didn't say very much.'

'I did. Didn't I? I didn't really know what to say. I answered the questions, didn't I? I guess I don't know. I've never done this before.'

'You kept looking over at me to check I was all right with what you were saying.'

'Did I? I suppose I wanted us to be – I don't know – for us to show a united front.'

'You have to tell her how you feel. Otherwise it won't work. There's no point going in there to show them how great our relationship is.'

'It's because of my memory, I think. I know I feel angry and hurt sometimes, but unless I'm actuallt feeling it in the moment, I forget.'

'It's good that we went.'

'Shall we go?'

I still have half my coffee left. 'Are we in a rush?'

'No. I just want to go.'

'Let me finish.' I take his hand. 'It's all right.'

'I know. I know it is. I just want to be somewhere else. To go and get the train and not be here anymore.'

W e are at the kitchen table on the laptop.
'Let's do Congo.'

Tomorrow, Tom goes to the Democratic Republic of Congo to work on a mapping project. I will be spending Christmas with Alice and her mum. His finger swipes land, grass and water away. Countries fly past. Green, blue, brown. River, landmass, sea. We zoom into a built-up area. He focuses in on Lubumbashi and tries to find the place where he will be staying. The poem that marks the spot is *affirming.shifters.imply.*

That afternoon I find a copy of Conrad's *Heart of Darkness* in a charity shop. Tom says he won't have time to read it, so I take it with me to the west coast of Wales.

Alice's mother's house is beside the sea and the beds and sofas are covered with home-made patchwork quilts. Nora and Alice's father met at university in Cardiff, but Nora is from Connecticut, where her American grandmother taught her how to quilt. After eating turkey and sweet potato, Alice and I go for a walk along the beach. The tide is far out and the pale sand glimmers in puddled stretches. The sky is the same greying white as the sea, making it impossible to tell where one ends and the other begins.

'I like this kind of beach,' I say. 'There is too much pressure when it's all blues and yellows.'

Alice looks out at the sea and nods. 'I think I know what you mean. All that pressure to be happy.'

Wren and Rose are with Richard this Christmas. When they Skyped this morning Alice had smiled into the screen and told Wren how much she loved her. Richard stayed off-camera and passed over various new toys. When Rose came on she mostly pretended to ignore her mother, but every so often blocked the whole screen with her ear as she tried to hug the computer.

'I can't believe he got Wren a new scooter too. I wish he'd discussed it with me first.'

'It must be so weird for Rose to see you on Skype.'

'Yeah, Fort-Da gone mad. I'm there, reminding her that I'm not there.'

I slip my arm through Alice's. Along the shining sand there are criss-crossing bare footprints. In the distance, there is the steep wall of the cliffs.

Nora's quilts are all intricately planned: tessellating hexagons and triangles, framed with further triangles or fanning out to form stars on bright white backgrounds. I tell her that they have a pilgrim-like look and she tells me that her family from way back were New England settlers. She was forty, she says, before she learnt what had really happened to the Indians.

'I cried so much when I read *Bury My Heart at Wounded Knee*.'

She shows me the quilt hanging in the hallway. It is the biggest in the house and the colours are bolder, not pastels like the others: elongated triangles make circles of orange against deep blue panels and there is a border of reds and purples. 'This one is for all those Indians that we tricked.'

Her daughter's wedding quilt was also large, a deeply ornate work of ivory and pearl. It had taken so much longer to complete than intended that its unveiling, instead of being on her first wedding anniversary, has coincided with her returning home to say she is getting a divorce.

Tom calls on WhatsApp, but we can't connect. I go outside and stand in the garden to try and get a signal.

'Can you hear me? It's really windy here.'

'Hello! What?' I walk away from the house.

'Can you hear me?'

'Yes.'

There is a long gap and then Tom says: 'Happy Christmas!'

There is whistling and a series of beeps. 'Are you there?'

'Wait while I . . .'

'Are you . . . What?'

'Wait for the gap or we'll both just be talking over each other.'

We both wait, then both begin speaking again at the same time. Tom tells me to go ahead.

'Happy Christmas,' I say. 'Are you having a good time?'

'I am. Are you?'

The whistling and beeping return.

'I don't want to talk like this.' I shout it into the empty landscape.

'Don't be angry. It's not personal. It's just the connection.'

'I know that.'

'Okay.'

The beeping returns and we lose the signal.

After the connection fails I stay standing outside, looking out over the stripes of estuary, field and sea. Something acidic and hot is moving through my veins. It's the same feeling as the one that used to fizz when I woke up in the night as a child, lying in the dark as shapes and presences loomed around the bed. Shadows pass over the silvery streaks below. I am fizzing now because I am afraid. And knowing that my fear is a response to something I am inventing makes it all the more scary. I put my phone back into my pocket.

We Skype later when I'm in bed.

'It's odd here. Like it's not even Christmas at all,' he says.

He has dark shadows under his eyes and the screen has him at a strange angle. I lean forward. 'Did you speak to your mum and dad?'

'Yeah, but the connection was bad.'

'Did you meet up with the other mapper?'

'Yes. He's a *natural mapper*. Meaning that he knows the location of villages because he's been there to visit patients, not because he knows how to read a map. We had to just agree that on the mobile phone, *north* means up.'

Tom, with only mediocre French, and Alan, with only basic English, had looked at the rough outline of the area they were trying to map. They were doing okay until Alan asked: *Qu'est-ce que north?*

'So, I take out my compass and I'm looking up the French words for *pole* or *magnet* or *bearing* or something on my phone – but then I realise that even if I can translate those words, I have no idea how to explain what they mean.'

He tells me that after lunch they had driven to the edge of Alan's geographical knowledge and Alan had asked a passer-by where to find the village chief. They had followed these directions to a building larger than most and found the chief squatting by the side of the road. Alan had squatted beside him and the chief had drawn a map in the sand showing the next three villages.

'Natural mapping. I like that,' I say.

'I thought you would.'

I look at the camera so it seems as if I'm looking into his eyes, then reach out and stroke his nose. His hand fills the screen in return.

On the train back home I read *Heart of Darkness*. I've not read it for years. Marlow's elegantly circling ruminations, page after page of beautiful description and ornate justification; the shock of that *Exterminate the brutes!* scrawled in Kurtz's notebook. Afterwards, I read the introductory essay by Chinua Achebe. *Can nobody see*, he asks, *the preposterous and perverse arrogance in thus reducing Africa to the role of props for the break-up of one petty European mind?*

I stare out of the window at the passing fields. The role of props. That's what I do. I collect fact after fact, story after story, but no matter what they are, they all sink into the same swamp: I ask everything the same question – what are you telling *me* about *me*? In every piece of news, in every horrible event in the plethora of horrible events, all I see is her, and me, and us –

Or is there something else? What if the answer that I am so selfish and so awful is just too easy? Too safe, and just another circling way to sink back into the swamp –

We are coming into the city, now. The two ugly blocks of flats rising up against the sky. It feels like a ridiculous thought – *who am I to even* – but I'm having it anyway: what if the shape or pattern that I can feel playing out in my life is worth thinking about? What if it's the same one that is shaping so much that is happening out there – a *dynamic* that I might be able to understand if only I could find a way to – find a way to –

The backs of brick houses and then suddenly, in the blue above them, a bright white vapour trail.

I t's January and Tom is sitting in the lounge reading *The Godfather*. Bright sunlight is coming through the window and the sound of drums and whistling is getting nearer. I look out: two police cars, six old men in military dress, six younger men in orange sashes, four drummers, three pipers and two flautists. They are marching down the street playing *When the Saints*. A few women in fancy hats and summer dresses follow along at the back. The song changes to *God Save the Queen*.

By the time I get outside, a few people have congregated beside the Orange Hall on the next road. There is a big man wearing robes and a ceremonial gold chain and a couple of drunk men are singing. The band halts outside the Golden Dragon Chinese take-away and the drummers raise a hand-sewn banner showing the face of John Knox. A woman in a bejewelled pink sari and carrying a foil-covered dish stands at the corner with three children in party dresses. They watch for a moment, then continue on towards the bus stop.

When I go back inside, the radio is on. *The time for empty talk is over. Now arrives the hour of action . . .* Trump is being inaugurated. *It's time to remember that old wisdom our soldiers will never forget. That whether we are black or brown or white, we all bleed the same red blood of patriots. We all dream the same dreams and are infused with breath by the same almighty creator.*

I first introduced Chloe to Sinead at a gallery. Sinead was wearing magenta lipstick, bright against her pale face. Her hair was up in a topknot and she stood in front of one of her own paintings. It's surface was off-white, made from peeling plaster and latex; the shapes drawn and painted into it were almost eyes, almost mouths, almost legs, arms, breasts and cocks.

I see Sinead in her studio all the time. I've never been there, but I can picture it. She is paint-splattered, we'll have her topless and in men's jeans. She wipes a hand on a bare breast to remove excess paint and continues to work on a picture she has never painted. She is, of course, whatever I am not.

When we were six, her windbreaker was pale yellow on top and white underneath. Between the two colours there was a thin line of brown trimming. Mine was pale green instead of yellow but otherwise identical. Occasionally, for fun, we would swap jackets. Her anorak, and me in it, had a nonchalance that mine lacked: a loose-limbed insouciance, a boyish shrug. The coat offered the possibility of decision through action rather than thought and, later, when I put mine back on I could feel the difference.

Sinead stood with one hand on her hip, the other holding a glass of white wine. I stood near the door with Chloe, who had come straight from work. She was stamping death certificates for the council back then, in an industrial park outside of town. She had quit her previous job as sustainability officer when it became clear she would mostly be laminating paper signs about recycling and coming up with initiatives to encourage people to switch their computers off at night. I led her over.

'Hey.'

Sinead sipped her wine. 'Well. If it isn't the return of the repressed.'

'Nice show.'

'Yeah.'

I motioned towards Chloe. 'This is Chloe. My girlfriend.'

Sinead's face paused for a beat. 'Okay. Interesting move.'

'Yeah. Well. Anyway. I just wanted to –'

'A substitution? This late in the game?'

'And what game is that?'

'Ah, yes. Innocence and amnesia. The old game-of-two-halves, same as ever. Well, nice to meet you. Chloe, was it?'

'Yeah. Hi.' Chloe half offered her hand, then, when it remained unshaken, retracted it. 'It's nice to – I like your –'

Sinead laughed. 'I bet you do.'

We all laughed a little then, but I wasn't sure why. I tried to find Sinead's eyes.

'So, how are things?'

Her laugh became loud and false. 'Spare me.' She turned to Chloe. 'You better keep your wits about you.'

'Okay,' I said. 'Let's not.'

'Indeed. Awkward. Difficult. Other people's problems.'

I shook my head and began to walk away, but then I looked back and caught a glimpse of her face. Her jaw had dropped, the cocky expression was gone and her eyes were wide. I gave Chloe an apologetic look.

'I told you she was crazy.'

In physics, twin particles form a quantum entanglement. Einstein called it *spooky action at a distance*. The two particles, because they were created in the same place at the same time, are described as having a shared existence – even if one particle is on a satellite in space and the other is on earth. You can't even describe them independently of one other: the only way to do it is by giving a *quantum state* for the pair as a unit.

You know when you are plugging in a monitor or laptop or something, plugging it in under a desk, one of those office desks with a hole for the wires? You've got one hand on top of the desk, where you can see it, and the other underneath, where you can't. You are passing the plug between them and one hand might touch the other without you intending it to. In yoga, there are moves that have the same effect. There is one where you sit cross-legged and put one hand over your shoulder and behind your back, the elbow pointing up. The other hand goes behind your back near the waist and reaches up. The two hands have to find each other behind you.

When Sinead and I touched ourselves together it was like that. We touched only ourselves, but our own hand was reaching into our own hot spaces to find the other's.

It smells like tomatoes.

Cooked tomatoes.

I'm right inside.

Me too. One side is softer than the other.

Something boney at the back.

Small fingers deep into vaginas and anuses. The running commentary, as if we were in a dark wet cave together without a torch.

Where are you?

I'm near the back.

It feels funny.

Now I'm in the funny bit too.

And then we are laughing, rolling around in our tent, our own hands curled inside us like tail-eating serpents. Other parts of the cave were not as funny. There were some places that made us feel sad or afraid.

It's like having no friends at all.

I don't like this bit. Let's go.

Laughing Cow cheese triangles, with sliced tomatoes, in a baguette. The whole cling-filmed sandwich hot from the sun. Sharp crumbs finding their way inside our spotted swimming costumes. Our teeth are wobbly, and under the pine trees, behind the beach, we play with the ones that are nearly ready to fall out, foreign objects swinging over dark cavities, hanging on only by tight red threads. All our wobbly teeth, four of them so far, have fallen out within two days of each other and have been in the exact same places. Now we are working on a back middle tooth on the right. A big one. I can get the tip of my finger underneath one side of it, making a delicious blunt pain on the other.

Can you do –

Yeah. And then –

Oh yeah. And if you –

Ow! Yeah.

The pale dusty ground is covered in long pine needles. We can feel them beneath our feet, knees and bottom. The smell is sweet and the light is sharply dappled; cold and dark in some spots, hot in others.

I can get my finger under it, in the hole!

How? Sinead hand moves toward my mouth. Her fingers touch my lip.

No.

What?

No.

What?

Her face is confused. I am shaking my head, my mouth closed. I can taste the iron taste that comes after we play with our teeth. She reaches again, touches my closed lips, drops her hand. It has gone quiet. A quiet we have never heard before. We are looking at each other.

'Well, I'll do it on my own tooth, then. I'll do it to myself.'

It's a different voice, coming from outside.

'I have a science question for you.'

I'm in bed and Chloe is getting undressed. Her eyes glint. She likes to be tested.

'How come, if me and my sister are genetically identical, she needed a brace and I didn't?'

Chloe pauses, her jeans half off. 'Because it's nature *via* nurture, not nature *versus* nurture.'

This was one of her favorite lines. 'Expand,' I say.

She drops her jeans and climbs out of them. 'Events happen in the environment to switch genes on and off. This means that things aren't determined, but as time passes and environments change, they become more or less probable. An environmental factor may have contributed to a chain of biological events that impacted the growth of your sister's teeth. Maybe she sucked her thumb more than you.'

I nod my head and raise my eyebrows. 'Ten points.'

She gets into bed beside me. 'Why are you thinking about that?'

'About what?'

'Your sister.'

'I'm not. It was just a question for you.'

But Chloe also has questions. These days she asks me what's wrong, why things aren't how they were in the beginning, why I don't seem to want to sleep with her anymore.

'I'm just tired.'

'You always say that.'

'What do you want me to say?'

'I want you to stop talking in riddles. Why can't you be honest with me?'

We are camping in Somerset, in Chloe's yellow two-man tent. My fingers are inside her and hers are inside me. It is becoming hot and blurry, harder to tell whose limbs belong to whom. We are breathing together when she lets out a moan that feels like it is coming from the inside of me. Suddenly, my inhale is hers, her exhale is coming out of my own lungs. As I turn, I see the ring of light that the

137

torch has made on the sloped yellow canvas, a translucent circle shining like a half-sucked fruit pastille. I pull away, but her hand is pushing further inside me, our legs tangled. I twist, we breathe, and then I have punched her in the face.

She reels back against the canvas and covers her nose.

'What?' There is confusion in her eyes. 'What just –'

The pyramid of tent is so small and she is lying between me and the exit. I can see her struggling to compute what has happened, starting to realise – I hit her again. There is scrambling. I have her hair in my fist. And then the zip and I am out.

III

T om goes away for work a lot more these days. He goes away, comes back and goes away again. Amsterdam, London, Brussels, Amsterdam. He opens the door, rucksack on his back, moustache growing down further over his top lip, and I feel nothing.

Then, later, I am sitting on the floor crying. 'It's like you've forgotten. Like you've forgotten everything. And it's not okay. It's not okay.'

I am sobbing now. He is on the sofa and has put his cup of tea down. 'But what have I forgotten?'

'You go and then you come back. And I don't know how to make us back together again. And it's as if you don't even notice. It's like you can't even tell the difference between what's real and what isn't.'

Stop the game. That's what we used to say: Stop the game, stop the game. Let's pretend, I say, and then you say, and then we . . .

Again, he says: 'You need to find a way to believe in me when I'm not here.'

I say: 'It keeps getting broken.'

He says: 'I can't keep starting from scratch again every time.'

He sits down on the floor beside me and pulls me in, but

when we start to kiss I say: 'How can I even kiss you with your moustache all long like that?'

When we first met, Tom's use of the word *sustainable* had loosened something. As I sat, tying myself in knots, he would say, it's not about whether it's good or bad, it's about whether it's sustainable or not. Now he says: The difference is, I think – so this is a relationship, and I wonder how it will be; you think, so this is a relationship – and it's like you've already decided what's going to happen.

I take the laptop into the kitchen, so I can put the vegetables in the oven while talking to him on Skype.

'A woman I'm working with has a saying,' he tells me. 'She's always saying it. Something like, it's not about the beads, it's about the string. Or, don't count the beads, follow the string.'

I sprinkle salt. 'Keep your eye on the prize and don't sweat the small stuff?'

'Big picture, little picture?'

I put the tray in. 'Done.'

'Hello, our kitchen.'

'What can you see?'

'The side of the counter, the olive oil, some wall and the edge of the door.'

I keep thinking about the meat factory where Mikal worked. The conveyor belt rolling on, a shadow stretching over the glistening fleshy portions. The metal lid lowers over whatever section of biochemical matter lies beneath it, then lifts, leaving the assemblage hermetically sealed in its own airtight pouch. The portion rolls on, ready to be labelled.

There is a smell and I think it's coming from the wardrobe. It reminds me of staying at our grandparents' house. There was an orange street light outside that shone through the curtains and we could hear high heels and shouting on the street outside. We lay together under the old electric blanket and on the wall opposite, next to a wardrobe that is just like ours now, there was a painting of the Sacred Heart.

The brightly coloured Jesus was pretty, but sad, painted in soft focus except for the graphically detailed gaping wound above his ribs. Tom and I found our wardrobe dumped by the bins outside the British Heart Foundation; one of the doors was hanging off, but Tom fixed it. It smells of dampness and pasts and it's worse when Tom is away.

The last step, on *Blue Peter*, was always to cover what you had made in sticky-back plastic. Under this final laminate layer, soggy card with glue-smeared edges and cheap crumbling pigment seemed to cohere, toilet rolls, ice-lolly sticks and other junk turning into something proper, something that had a name.

W hen I was twenty and in bed with the second boy I ever slept with, I found myself curled in a ball under the blankets. One moment his cock was edging its way towards my closed thighs, the next I had dived under the duvet. To his credit he joined me there and asked what was wrong. My own answer came as a surprise to me:

'Something happened with my sister.'

I had my eyes closed, but I could feel he was still there. I kept my eyes closed and felt the heat rising. *What the fuck is wrong with you? What the fuck. Now he is going to see. Now he is going to know.*

'What do you mean? What happened with your sister?' His voice was kind, but I knew from experience that kindness has a shelf life. If a problem takes too long to solve, it becomes your own fault. *You need to get over yourself. You need to get over yourself now.* I open my eyes.

'Forget it. Let's just do it.'

I straightened out and he climbed on top of me to arrange things. 'You need to open your knees.'

'I am.'

'You're not.'

I liked that man. It wasn't that I didn't want to, whatever *wanting* might have meant back then. After intercourse was technically achieved, we sat up, leaning our heads on the poster of *The Crow* that hung above his mattress.

I had watched this man take out the bins at the bar where we both worked and had felt a flicker of spontaneous feeling. An actual, unprompted sensation in my actual body – that was the first miracle. A week later, when I was on shift again, he came in with a book and sat reading at a table in the corner. That was the second miracle: a man who would read in public. Wiping the table next to his, I asked what he was reading for and he got it.

'It didn't seem like you wanted to.'

'I did. I do.'

He was cross. 'I could hardly get your legs open.'

'I told you. It's . . .'

But I didn't have the words to explain. Didn't even know what it was I wanted to explain. How does that happen? How do you end up, at twenty, with an absolute absence of words to describe your own life?

What three words? What3words describe the consensual, shareable description of my specific location? What tiny post-human poem, what spell, will offer me my own longitude and latitude?

Before we broke up, the second man I slept with went to the corner shop to buy bread. While he was gone, I filled the kettle, put it on the hob and paced around his kitchen, not thinking about another boy's kitchen I had paced around in the early morning, whispering down the phone to Mum. Her words, *Sinead's in the hospital*. Me thinking, of course she is. Hanging up, silently gathering my shoes and bag and closing the door behind me. Feathers singeing. The smell of burning was pretty strong before I noticed the kettle was on fire. I threw it into the sink and turned on the cold tap. The black plastic around the electric socket hole had melted into a bulbous lump.

It stank in the sink as we ate toast and jam and he told me he didn't think this was going to work.

'I don't think it's meant to be that difficult.'

'Right. Yeah.'

'I mean, like, it's supposed to be fun.'

'I guess I'm just not very . . .'

He went over to the sink and leaned over it to open the window even wider. 'I need to be with someone more –'

I wasn't going to let him finish that sentence. 'It's fine. No problem. Sorry I melted your kettle.'

As he was turning back around, I thought about taking a step towards him and putting my hand on his face, kissing his mouth. But how would a person do a thing like that? How might a person even begin to become the kind of person who would know how to do a thing like that?

'Stupid fucking copy kettle copying a kettle,' I said.

'Yeah.'

It's summer and busy at work. More children's birthday parties means more blowing up of helium balloons and more wiping up of cake vomit. Trump is building his wall, Italy is paying the Libyans to stop migrant boats and the UK far-right are trying to prevent rescue missions in the Med. They have started a crowdfunding campaign – £56,489 so far – for more ships and filming equipment. There is a lot about fascism in the news, headline after headline asking if we are going back to the 1930s.

The phenomenon of noticing something and then seeing it everywhere is called a frequency illusion. It is also called the Baader Meinhof phenomenon. But how do we know when this feeling of something being spoken of everywhere is a cognitive bias and when it is the slow detection of an underlying pattern? And then there's the story of the Baader Meinhof gang itself: the Red Army Faction – a violent protest group in 1970s West Germany – were reacting to the fact that so many ex-Nazis still held power. They saw themselves as continuing the war against fascism. They themselves were caught up in a different kind of illusion: same-thing/different name; different-thing/same-name.

I realise that beyond the superficial markings I'm not even sure what the definition of fascism is. Hitler, Mussolini, yes, but I'm not sure how I'd really define it. I go on Wikipedia. I read about *protectionism and forging of national unity to maintain a stable and orderly society*; about *no clear line between the public and the private sphere*; *a system of government arranged around corporate power*. There is also a quote from a historian saying that in the past *regimes that were not functionally fascist borrowed elements of fascist decor in order to lend themselves an aura of force and vitality*. I still feel like I'm missing something.

I also think a lot about Chloe these days. After our camping trip, after we broke up, I moved into a house with a couple I didn't know. Every evening they curled up together on the sofa to eat pizza and watch cooking shows, then after she went to bed he stayed up till the early hours to play *Call of Duty*. My bedroom was on the ground floor, right next to the lounge, and I would lie awake till almost dawn, looking out at the silent street through a lace-curtained bay window, listening to gunfire, pounding footsteps and howling.

I saw a therapist for a little while back then. He was pretty old-school: mostly silent, except for the occasional *And what do you think that means?* It quickly became clear that for him, what it usually meant was the incubator. This got boring and after a few months I left. I couldn't work out what he wanted me to learn from my neonatal experience besides the obvious: never again let yourself become so utterly helpless and perilously close to death; never again put yourself into a position where strangers can insert things into your orifices with impunity.

Sinead and I were never very good at sharing a bed after the tooth incident. When we stayed at our grandparents, we'd always start off establishing the rules. Even at seven, we knew trial-and-error was for other people; we knew about the undertow and the speed of that slippery slope. A line down the middle of the sheet would be carefully drawn with a finger and territories established. Regardless, good intentions always turned sour. Within the hour, blood pounding, gripping our respective sides of the blanket, we'd be kicking out as hard as we could; thighs, knees and toes meeting soles of feet. The clash of shins and no way to stop it now; bruised and crying and kicking on.

Grandad was rolling his eyes and speaking to Dad.

'Look at them. Like a couple of Pakis. Talking away to themselves. No one else can understand a word they say.'

With his mouth, Dad says, Girls, come on, stop messing around and talking to yourselves. With his eyes, he says, As you know, that is not a nice word and not one you should use. There is a short pause before transmission restarts: I am not going to say anything to Grandad about it because – eye contact cuts out and the rest of the message is lost.

To follow the tracks of an animal you have never seen, you have to ask yourself how it would behave here, in these particular woods. Then you must imitate those actions and follow whatever traces such behaviour might leave.

Chloe is sat on the toilet, baggy pale grey pyjama bottoms around her ankles and a soft blue long-sleeved top, the sleeves pushed up. Her dark hair is tangled and straggly and her expression is one of complete unselfconsciousness. Her elbows are bent, her forearms resting on her thighs, her hands loose between her bare legs. I am at the sink, toothbrush in hand, watching her.

Her chin is pushed forward slightly, a nonchalant waiting. She is almost whistling. Her nose is ever so slightly wrinkled. She is, at that moment, nothing but herself, pissing. That. *That* is who or what I want. Not the one who stands and wipes and pulls up her pyjamas, asks me if I want toast. But what does *want* even mean? To lift her off the toilet, throw her on the bed and put my face in her piss-damp hair, pyjamas still around her ankles?

I had the toothbrush in my mouth but I wasn't brushing. I was watching her sitting there. I wanted to wrap my arms around her. Wrap my arms around her sleep-stinky bones, cheek still indented with sheet, shoulders shrugged and hands dangling. I turned and bent towards her. She moved her face, a strand of hair falling over her eye.

'Not while I'm on the toilet.'

'You're sexy when you're on the toilet.'

But she had changed now, her back straighter, another expression masking whatever had been there before.

She shook her head and I turned back to the mirror and began to brush. After she left, I stood there looking at the half-drunk glass of tap water on the shelf above the sink. It'd been there all week, clouding and growing bleachy bubbles.

We were sitting in Chloe's back yard. At end of it the motorway ran between the street and the sky; a horizon with traffic flowing across it. We were talking about her *Xenopus* frogs.

'They're dichromatic,' she told me. 'They change colour during mating season. They also change when they're anxious.'

We were drinking red wine and I was already on my third glass. 'So why was that one still black when all the others had gone white?'

In the lab that afternoon one of the frogs had failed to change colour. I'd shouted, Quick! We need to help it! and Chloe had looked at me like I'd gone mad.

'I told you. It was proably blind.' She started to sing. '*He didn't notice that the lights had changed.*'

'Stop it.

'Why are you so upset about it?'.

'Because it looked afraid. And they could all see. They could all see that there was something wrong with him and he didn't even know. Didn't even know and they could all see.'

'You know these are frogs, right? Very limited capacity for self-consciousness.'

'I just *felt* for him.'

'Of course you did.'

148

The next morning, Chloe was standing in her narrow galley kitchen, washing up. Behind her, the row of hanging saucepans flashed in the sunlight. The door from the kitchen to the yard was open and I could see the plastic chairs we'd sat on last night, one lying on its side beside the broken wine bottle. Close your eyes, she used to say about the motorway traffic, and it sounds like the sea. As I walked towards her, she looked up and said she was going to have breakfast in the garden. Her voice went up, almost imperceptibly, at the end of the sentence.

Last night, after I'd accused her of thinking that I was like that blind frog, she'd rolled her eyes.

'Right. Because all our experiments on the African clawed frog are really about *you*.'

She was looking at me like I was mad again. 'You think I'm crazy.'

'I never said that.'

'You think I'm crazy and banging my head against the fucking tank.'

'What are you talking about?'

I stood up. 'Just don't look at me like that.'

I used to get so frustrated, so angry, so quickly. And then she told me I should try and stay calm.

Y ou can get videos of twins fighting inside the womb now. On YouTube, in 4D technology, you can see the bigger twin sucking on a tube while the smaller one kicks at her with a tiny foot. Small but repeated kicks as the bigger one tries to eat – kick kick, suck suck suck. This goes on for a while, until after a pregnant pause the bigger one twists, swings back an arm and smacks her twin in the face.

Her sitting on the floor between Dad's feet, me waiting with wet hair against the radiator.

'Look how lovely and silky my hair is now. Look how lovely and silky my hair is now.'

Sinead and I talked a lot on the phone that first year, when we were both still at art college, before everything happened. I remember one conversation in particular because we had it the night before I went home with Adam.

My university halls were built around a large car park; the rooms had the thin blue carpet of a call centre and windows that didn't open. I was outside on the doorstep, the spiral telephone cord pulled taut from the socket in the hall.

Sinead was always full of exciting stories. 'It's amazing. I'm having such a good time. It's like, now I can finally be who I am, rather than the one everyone always said I was.'

'That's good. I don't know if I'm having that good a time.'

'Why not?'

'Things feel kind of empty.' Twisting the telephone cord and looking out at the concrete. A couple of students were smoking beside a car and I could hear Oasis' *Champagne Supernova* coming from one of the windows. 'Maybe I'm not having a good time because you're having all the good times.'

'Maybe.'

I 'm talking to Alice on the phone. I tell her about a conversation I once had with my mum.

'I was trying to explain how awful it was growing up and she just smiled and said, But don't you see, it's only because you see one another as part of yourselves that you treat each other like that.'

I also tell her that Tom and I went to see the therapist.

'Why?'

'Stuff.'

'Did it help?'

'We filled out a questionnaire. But they were the wrong questions.'

Later, we are laughing about Wren. Alice is worried that she already has a penchant for self-harm: sticking plasters in their house are Peppa Pig-themed and she has been known to purposefully injure herself to be awarded one. I can hear her in the background, shouting.

'Wait a minute, Wren. Mummy's talking on the phone.' On the other end of the line, there is shuffling. Wren is saying that she needs the purple one and there is the sound of things being arranged.

'You're so calm,' I say.

'Well, I guess it makes sense to stay calm right now.'

'How d'you mean?'

'When I'm going mad with lack of sleep, I just tell myself that it's only for a few years, I just need to stay calm for a few years and it'll be worth it in the long run.'

'I know, but – how can you hold on to that sense of perspective, in the very moment?'

'Well, like I say. It makes sense in the long run.'

'You are so good at believing in the future. It's like with

Tom, I already can't believe how long it's lasted, that it's still okay. The longer it goes on, the more afraid I get.'

'Of what?'

'Of what's to come, I guess. Of when it all inevitably goes to shit. Whenever he comes back after being away, I freak out. It's like I'm terrified he'll come back different, like it will have all disappeared and he'll have realised he doesn't love me anymore.'

Tom comes home from his latest trip covered in scabs. He came off a motorbike while travelling to a far-flung village. Flesh is visible in a hole in his hand and both of his forearms and knees are red. It's early in the morning and I am still in bed. He gets into the warmth beside me, holding up both arms so as not to have the duvet rub against his skin. When I take his hand, he cries out, so I put my hand on his chest, inside his T-shirt, instead.

'I think we'll probably break up soon,' I say

'What? Why are you saying that?'

'It's just going to happen. At some point you'll realise I'm not really who you think I am.'

'Do I even get a say in this?'

'You're an optimist. You like to think we'll be okay. But I'm a realist.'

He shakes his head and crosses his arms over his chest, still protecting his scabs. 'That's not what you are at all. You know, sometimes I don't even feel like you're even talking to me; it's like you're really talking to your sister or your dad or something. It's like I'm not even here.'

'I'm not doing that. Am I doing that? Why would I do that?'

I get up and go to the kitchen. I watch the kettle boil and look at Facebook. My Canadian friend of a friend from long ago has posted a picture of her three boys. Photographed from the back, they are looking out the window at their snow-covered driveway. They all have short shaggy brown hair, but each one also has a very thin long blond plait hanging down his back. A tiny section of their hair kept uncut since birth. Tom comes into the kitchen.

'Let's not fight. I just got home. Sometimes it just feels like you're putting me into this strange box.'

'I'm sorry. Let's forget it.'

'You worry too much. We have to let the future happen.'

I pour the water into the cafetiere and agree. We decide to go somewhere, do something nice together. We book tickets to go to a small music festival later in the summer.

There are two donated birthday cakes on the table at the shelter. One is green, with football-pitch markings and *Happy 50th Birthday Harry* in white; the other is blue and has the words *Over the Hill* in a curly script above *Happy Birthday Roy*. A new influx of younger men has arrived, lively and Arabic-speaking. Samir has asked me to read a crumpled copy of a chapter from his PhD thesis called *Strategies for Finance and Investment in Libya*. He wants me to check he has formatted his references correctly. I read it; he has. One of the most pressing issues, the paper argues, is that Libya no longer presents a reliable investment opportunity.

I watch a documentary on the BBC. It is filmed on mobile phones and documents Syrians crossing the Aegean Sea, then travelling on through Europe. In the Turkish port of Izmir, shops that used to sell tourist tat now sell life jackets and waterproof phone pouches. Multicoloured buoyancy aids hang outside stalls, like beach toys, with shop assistants letting families try things on, offering them advice on style and fit.

I watch another video online. This one shows a large man standing next to a bin. He holds a bunch of uninflated balloons. They are party balloons with a coloured cartoon character printed on them. He is talking in Turkish and stretching them.

An English voice behind the camera says, 'How does it work?'

'To keep phone dry.'

'Show me.'

The man separates a yellow balloon from the bunch. The frame and image shake, then the picture goes completely yellow. It remains yellow for a few seconds, then the yellow recedes and the phone is out, the man back beside the bin, stretching the balloon between his hands.

Taha has now been housed, but many of the men I met on my first night at the shelter remain. Their faces are growing more drawn, and they repeat the rules crossly to the noisy newcomers. Men come in and cut large wedges of fondant-iced sponge. Some ask, Who is this Harry? or say, *Şükran*, Roy!

Did Harry and Roy die before their birthdays? Did someone forget to go to the supermarket to pick up their cakes? The news moves on to the next story. I watch the men watch men in an inflatable dinghy approach a beach. The captions are still lagging behind the pictures, the transcription for the previous news segment – Trump's firing of the US FBI director – isv still running along the bottom of the screen. Footage of men clambering out of a dinghy, lifting children and wading through the waves. A pregnant woman, bent over, staggering to the shore, wailing.

The news moves on to a scene of flowers piled up at London Bridge for the victims of last month's attack. The lagging caption reads *and more will continue to make the perilous journey.*

W e are driving to the festival in the rain. Tom moves his hand from wheel to gearstick and when I put my hand on top of his, he smiles. I watch his feet, down there in the dark, pressing the pedals. I did take a driving lesson, once. It was with Mum, in her old Peugeot 305.

It was a few weeks after Sinead came out of hospital and we were both living back at home again. I got into the driving seat and Mum went through the pedals and gears, showing me which did what.

'Why don't you try turning the key? Good. That's the engine switched on.'

She explained the handbrake and something about the front lights. If you wanted to start moving, she said, you'd slowly lift your foot up off the clutch and slowly press the other foot down on the accelerator.

While she was showing me this, Sinead had come out and was standing in the drive wearing jeans and my blue shirt, standing with her back to the low wall that separated the driveway from the footpath. Between her and the wall was Mum's border of tulips and marigolds. I hadn't seen her dressed for a while. Those days she was mostly in her bedroom or the kitchen, crying, her face red and her hair matted, wearing her dirty USSR T-shirt, the green one with a red star on it. Standing in the kitchen while the rest of us tried to get on with things, crying about how everything had fallen apart, about how she couldn't go on.

'You move the gearstick into first gear.'

I did this.

'Then you lift your foot very slowly until you feel the biting point. Can you feel it?'

I could. I held it there and felt it vibrating.

We arrive at the festival and I wait for the toilet in the drizzle. In the queue with me is a tiger in a thin onesie and a man in neon orange shorts, a feather boa, a top hat and a beard. There is also a woman in a sequinned dress and Hunter wellies who is carrying a chicken's head made out of wet cardboard.

The fairy lights are flickering on at the food stalls and a large pile of wood for the bonfire is circled by a ring of torch lanterns and sodden haystacks. We are not far from the sea and there are seagulls scraping over bones and rot. It is raining more heavily now and people huddle under trees or walk fast, hoods up, heading for somewhere dry.

As we queue for burgers under a dripping awning, we scroll through Twitter on Tom's phone. Men in Charlottesville, USA, have been marching with guns and banners reading *Unite the Right* and *White Knights KKK*. The

Confederate flag is being carried alongside swastikas. There are reports of men chanting *You Will Not Replace Us.*

'Oh, wow. And someone has driven a car into the protesters.'

'Which protesters?' I ask.

'The anti-fascists.'

I keep my eyes on the chalkboard beside the serving hatch. Extra toppings of cheddar, blue cheese, jalapeño or fried onions. 'A car? They drove a car at them?'

'Yeah. A woman is dead. Thirty-two. Jesus. Why would someone do that?'

I stare at the falafel van a little further along. A man is wearing a purple wetsuit, a gold scuba-diving mask and a tie with Santa Claus on it. Fuck.

The first time Sinead and I saw a Magic Eye picture was downstairs in the local shopping centre. We stood in front of it and tried to see the hidden image. After we had stood there for a while, looking at it and at each other, the man running the stall said, Don't try so hard and you have to squint. We were twelve and the pictures were at the height of their fame.

Suddenly, Sinead shouted, 'I can see it! It's a car!' She was pointing at the poster.

'Ha ha! Can you see it? Look! It's there, right in the middle!'

I stared harder, but I couldn't see anything except the psychedelic pattern. 'Where? How do you do it?'

Sinead was clapping her hands. 'We should buy one!'

'Wait! I can't see anything!'

All of a sudden and there it is. The car. I can see it, and I know that I know the answer to Tom's question. Once the image appears, hanging there in all its 3D glory, you can't go back to not seeing it: can't go back to not knowing why someone would drive a car as fast as they could at someone. Can't go back to not knowing that you know you know you know.

I want to get away from the people and the noise. We walk from the festival site into a wooded area and keep walking until we arrive at the remains of a fire. A charred branch on the sandy mud, the shells of two eggs and a scattering of small white feathers. Three blackened bottles of deodorant, one split open.

'What a weird feast,' Tom says.

We move around the remnants. Tom picks up a stick and pokes one of the warped deodorant cans. I can read the names on two of them. *Total Defence* and *Stress Protect*. We sit on a fallen trunk and are quiet. I turn the last deodorant can over with my foot. *Soft and Gentle*.

Suddenly Tom is telling me a story about being a Scout. He was thirteen and on a trip organised by a group of older Venture Scouts. The younger boys stayed alone in a cabin somewhere in the Highlands and did orienteering tasks set for them by the older boys. There was a night-time treasure hunt where at every grid reference there was a tin box containing the next clue. The Gulf War had begun a few months before and many of the Scouts' tasks were war-based. In one, the boys had to set off fireworks to blow up an enemy weapons dump and in others, they had to hide to avoid capture. After the blast, they made a fire, boiled water in their Trangia and had tea with custard creams.

Tom is poking at *Soft and Gentle* with a stick as he talks. I can't see his face inside the hood of his waterproof. I'm thinking of that black-and-white image of little Bob Gore-Tex junior and his camping bag. I saw it in a video I watched ages ago, when I was buying my new cagoule. Bob in a Scout uniform, with a waterproof camping pack and transparent plastic tent, designed by his dad and sewn by his mum.

'Naked women on every surface. Even the cupboards. It was kind of frenzied, like we were all high. The pictures were everywhere.'

I'm listening again. Tom is telling me how, when the boys arrived back at the cabin late that night, after the treasure hunt, they had switched on the lights and found the walls and ceiling all covered in pictures of women.

'What kind of porn?' I ask.

'You know. *Razzle*. *Hustler*. Pretty grimy, lots of make-up, women looking over their shoulders like they really want you to fuck them. The whole room. It was all spread legs and shaved cunts. Women bent over and looking up as they sucked cock.'

'What did you do?'

'I guess we just looked. Some boys didn't like it and got in their sleeping bags to go to sleep. It got a bit crazy. We ended up dragging this one boy out of bed in his sleeping bag and dumping him in the river.'

'Why? Why put the boy in the river?'

Tom toes the scraps of kindling at his feet. 'It all felt so exciting. There was this rush. But, at the same time, this other feeling. A kind of anger at the boys who didn't want to look and had got into bed. I guess there must have been this sense of being judged, some kind of shame or guilt, as well as all the excitement. It was me who started it. I started going on at this one guy, Simon. Telling him to come and look at this picture, a woman's ass being held open. I kept saying, What, are you scared? and things like that. Then we were dragging him out of his bed in his sleeping bag, out of the door and down to the river. The water was shallow and it wasn't far. Maybe a hundred feet away. But that was exciting too. It was the same kind of excitement.'

'Why are you telling me this story now?'

He takes down his hood. 'I don't know.'

'Because of Charlottesville?'

'I don't know.'

That YouTube moment of Gore-Tex Bob pulling the rod. One sudden movement and one thing becomes something else, an entirely new physical substance.

'I had a driving lesson once.' I say it fast, looking straight ahead.

'You did?'

'With my mum. Sinead came out while we were doing it. Into the front drive.'

Mum shouting something and the sudden speed. Sinead's face and Mum reaching wildly for wheel.

'I put my foot on the accelerator and drove right at her.'

I can feel us ending. I turn to face him. His expression shifts to neutral, but I see what was there before. It's over.

L itter is churned into mud tracks and seagulls stutter and hop, squawking their horrible call of *mine mine mine*. I watch two men in tuxedos drink from cans as a woman in a muddy ball gown laughs beside them. I walk around the back of the bar tent. There are bins and bin-bags overflowing in the mud, and more seagulls pecking at them. One moment it's a party, but turn a corner and it's fucking Calais. Through the screen and into the parallel world, where everything is turned the other way round.

The words *All You Need Is Love* have been painted in 70s bubble-letter font on the canvas. I hit Chloe for the same reason that I pushed my foot down on the gas. It felt like she was making me disappear, so I made her disappear instead. I drove the car straight at Sinead. If she hadn't thrown herself over the wall, I'd have smashed into her instead of it. I am the driver at the protest and the one in the Channel Tunnel. I am the marchers shouting *You Will Not Replace Me*.

Cans and smashed glass are sticking out where the tent meets the grass. *Lieu de Vie* painted onto the sides of tents in the jungle. *Place of life*. I lean against the canvas. They were counting on legal arguments using article twenty-five of the Universal Declaration of Human Rights. The decree that *dwelling places* can't be destroyed.

The smell of wet tent and Chloe's face after I hit her. The smell of my panic, and hers, filling that tiny damp space. Her face. Shock shifting into hurt and then anger. But also something else. Something in her eyes that said *I knew it*. Hitting her again, then the squalling mess of feet and knees as I scrambled through the flap, hopping into my pants outside the tent, falling over, then running bare-foot to the road beyond the campsite entrance.

Don't tell me the moon is shining, show me the glint on broken glass. Chloe used to quote Chekhov whenever a seagull passed over our heads at night. The way their wings caught the moon, the up-lit white glow as they glided above, the rest of their species stumbling blindly below. We were walking home through town when she delivered her line to me for the last time.

'*Don't tell me the moon . . .*'

'Right. And, *Beauty is Truth and Truth Beauty.*'

'Exactly.' She warmed quickly to her theme. 'Science is about truth in the specifics – about the truth of an exact detail and precise moment. And in being true, all things become beautiful.'

'Except that the truth isn't beautiful.'

'It is. It's beautiful because it exists. Even if the moment is ugly and awful – in the very fact that it *is*, there is a beauty.'

'No. The truth isn't fucking beautiful. If you think it is, then you know nothing about people, about life – about the logic of – about what makes people – about anything.'

What had she said after that? Something about me not seeing the bigger picture, not wanting to understand what she was saying.

I had stood outside the campsite, me, again, as the blind flailing fucking frog. I could hear a car in the distance. I wrapped my arms around myself. I was standing nearly naked by the side of the road. *This moment exists.* This moment is therefore beautiful? I now had to crawl back into that tent as the person who just did what I just did and doesn't even know why. The car was getting closer. I began to walk back towards the tent.

Sinead's small warm body beside me in a different tent. The canvas is pulled taut like an animal hide, covered in wet handprints and scratches. Words written on, rubbed off, rewritten, re-rubbed. Time passes, but that which was pumiced away starts to show through. Iron from old ink oxidises and rust-red words begin to appear. A line you drew long ago: on one side is everything that is bad, on the other side, an idea of yourself so tenuous and so untrue that you must spend the rest of your life protecting it.

I go into the bar. It is hot with bodies, smelling of warm wet grass and sweat. I fight through and buy a double whisky. A couple next to me are talking about Charlottesville. Tiki, the brand of garden-party torch that men were carrying on the march, have just released a statement. The woman is reading to the man from her phone: *We do not support their message or the use of our products in this way. Our products are designed to enhance backyard gatherings and to help family and friends connect with each other at home in their garden.* I drink another whisky. The music is getting louder. People are laughing and people are shouting. My throat is warm and my head feels light. I walk back out. Sudden cool air. And then I see Tom.

It has to be in spite of.
    I used to say this all the time when Tom and I were

first getting together. We would go on a date and I would get faint with what I claimed was hunger. We would have to walk quietly and slowly and sometimes I would cry. What's wrong? he would ask. It's nothing, I'm just hungry, I'd say. He began carrying cereal bars.

That bodes well.

That's something he used to say. When good things happened to us, when we happened upon unexpected co-incidences or shared pleasures. Yes, it bodes well, I'd say, but I want us to be in spite of. I didn't even know what I meant, but he agreed. Yes, he'd say, in spite of, in spite of everything.

Guitars and bass are reverberating from inside the tent and Tom is standing beside the bin, beside the binbags, beside the seagulls. I walk towards him. *Mine mine mine.* I call out his name but then I see that there is someone else there. Someone standing much closer to him than she should be. *Clattering, clattering, clattering weapons.* He is kissing her. Not just kissing her but pressed up against her. One hand down the back of her jeans, the other on her face. I feel his cock pressed up against me, my thighs parting and his tongue deep inside my mouth.

Then I'm throwing up, sick all over the grass, all over the rubbish. Orange sick with gristly grey lumps. I retch again. Her smile – his hand down the front of her jeans now, in the hair, opening her lips. She is watching me watching her over his shoulder as the feeling spreads through both of us.

I sit on the bus and hold my mind very still. I let myself think about the shape of the island we saw from Portobello beach. Talking about fake collective nouns and fake life jackets. Without even going back to our tent to get anything I had got on the first coach leaving the festival. When we pulled into Edinburgh station, the destination on the bus in the next bay along was *Forth Bridge*. Ferries set sail from there out to the islands. I took it as a sign and got on.

Anxiety is measured on a continuum and learnt in an associative manner. In the lab, with rats, it is measured through aversion and inhibition; using booby-trapped mazes, scientists measure it by assessing the degree to which rats avoid novel items and lack spontaneous action. Measuring identity is more difficult: they say it's a case of continuum, association, performance and sedimentation. To exist we must be recognised and, to be recognised, we must be readable; the less prone we are to the spontaneous or the unclassifiable, the more our existence is conferred.

I stare out of the window as the bus makes its way to the Firth of Forth. A yellow crane, squat cylindrical cooling towers. Graffiti in green, purple and grey, and the sky getting pinker. A reflection of a reflection as another coach passes us; a flash of ghost-coach and then gone. Tall beige ferns and russet cut bracken. A red digger lifts its bucket and tips earth onto a pile. Two mounds of rusting washing machines and fridges; a white goods mass grave.

If the brain really uses the past to make your reality, a simulation based on what happened before – but that simulation too must have been only a simulation, a simulation based on what you had thought was happening before that – a Möbius strip, a looping, looping loop –

In fight or flight situations, the brain goes into panic mode. Communication between body and brain stops functioning properly. This is when we need to resort to the glucocorticoid system. That's right. The one all that rat-licking switches on. Without that system in good working order, able to restore equilibrium, the panic just loops on exponentially, more cortisol and adrenaline making more cortisol and adrenaline –

A dead deer, they say, has exactly enough brains to tan its own hide. Coating the fibres with brain fluid prevents deterioration. After it is brained, the hide needs to dry out; it must then be beaten to loosen its fibres, then smoked. Remove the deer brains and mash with warm water to make a thick paste.

The website where I read these hide-tanning instructions recommended using your blender to make a daiquiri-like solution. It is unclear what geodemographic commercial segment fresh-daiquiri-making-animal-skinners would be classified as. Cafés and Catchments? Streetwise Single? Golden Retirement? Cut around both hind feet, then slit the backs of the legs open to the anus. Add rum, sugar, lime and ice to blend.

A red traffic light. Clouds of steam rising from somewhere like smoke. The bus passes the McVitie's factory, a corrugated-iron warehouse stamped with the words *You'd have to go a long way to find a better biscuit.*

Well, Dad used to say, that's just the way the cookie crumbles. Is it true that there are researchers at a university somewhere doing research into that? *Digital speckle pattern interferometry,* I think it was. Studying changes in the structure of biscuits as they heat and cool. Monitoring tiny deformations and patterns to detect stress and prevent breakages. Good, as always, to know what is materially possible.

We have a tea towel with the Periodic Table printed on it. We? A tea towel. Lovely and colourful. The actinides are that nice duck-egg blue, the kind you'd use to paint a vintage dresser. The actinides are all radioactive; either isotopically unstable or entirely artificial. On the middle right, where the lanthanides meet the transition metals, there is a red stain that Tom thinks is tomato sauce. Further to the right, covering the nobel gases of krypton and xenon, are darker, brown markings of unknown origin. The tea towel declares itself to be *For Institutions of Empirical Learning.*

Just before my phone runs out of battery, I see the breaking news: *Trump responds to Charlottesville Rally: I think there's blame on both sides. If you look at both sides – I think there's blame on both sides. And some very fine people on both sides.*

Now I'm on the ferry, leaning out over the side and gasping, rocking up and down and up and down, seeing the dark waves, then throwing up again.

I step off the boat, bend over and puke onto the grass. I wipe my mouth on the back of my sleeve and watch the ferry plough away towards the mainland, churning the water up behind it. Before me, a grey sky and a grey sea; behind me, a yellow lighthouse atop a wet green hill. No sound, except the waves and the wind. *The thin place.*

Silence. I stand still and let it wash over me. Silence, except for the sound of the sea, and, beyond that, the caw of a bird. The wind in the grass. All I have with me is a dead phone and a W. H. Smith bag with supplies that I bought at the bus station: a box of matches, a bottle of Glenfiddich, six packets of oatcakes, a packet of shortbread fingers and a large bag of salted peanuts.

I open the bottle of whisky and take a swig. Yes, in this thin place something will happen. This is the place where something will change, where all the pieces will come together. A grey sea and a grey sky. Like Turner's *Calm Sea with Distant Grey Clouds*. A sketch of nothing at all; smears of white and grey paint, scratches of a pale yellow, a faint line of faded brown. A painting that was at once an abstract work and a precise, accurate depiction of its titular scene. Whisky, whisky, whisky.

Up ahead, the lighthouse, and down the hill on the left another structure, an old house or barracks. I'll go there. Make a fire. Drink my whisky and eat my peanuts. Bring it on. But, no. First, I'll swim. That cold shock. And then, afterwards, that feeling of being different. New. On the other side of the island I can see a loch, floating silver in the distance. I'd wade in and, yes. Become someone new. Someone else. Wade in and know what to do.

When I reach it, the loch is small and has a thick low white mist floating above it. On one side is the cliff edge and, beyond it, the sea again. I take off my clothes and stand naked looking out. *This moment. This moment is true and therefore – this moment matters – this is the moment where –*

There is a smell and it is getting stronger. Suddenly, wet, white and furry, something touching my foot. I yell and step back. A goat's body emerges from the mist, scruffy and with one of my boots in its mouth. I grab for the boot and the goat lurches forward. I jump back.

'Get away!'

It startles and begins to run, my boot still in its mouth. I grab my jumper and the other boot and hurtle after it, the stony ground tearing at the soles of my feet.

'Stop. Fuck. Wait!'

The goat is running towards where the land starts to fall sharply down towards the cliff. I pick up a rock and throw it. Then another. Eventually one hits the goat on the side. It yelps and stops. I shove my bare foot into the boot I still have and hop wildly in its direction. As I approach, it starts to move off again. I throw myself at the boot and yank it. The goat keeps its grip. With my shod foot I kick out at it. It skips its hind legs up to avoid me. I kick again, this time the toes of my boot meeting its stomach hard. It squeals but keeps hold of the boot. I kick again, harder, and then again. On my fifth or sixth kick, it drops it, limping away.

I slump onto the ground, pulling my boot in towards my chest.

I sit on the grass, naked but shod, and listen to the sound of the sea. Alice's mother would know what to do. That quilt she made for Wren. Something so pretty out of all those scraps. I remember crying on the phone to my mum after Chloe and I had just broken up. I had told her that I didn't know how to love properly, that I didn't know what to do. She was quiet for a while, then she said something that was so unlike her. She said, There's no such thing as properly. It sounded like a kind of forgiveness. I wrapped my jumper around me. I needed to try and think things through.

Tom. We'd found each other again behind the bar tent. He was pushing me up against the bin, his hand down my jeans, between my legs. A sore-throat locket sucked and cracking, hot honey flowing out. Flowing hot and nothing but a voice saying, go with this, do this. Forget everything else and be in this moment. I had my face in his neck and we were pressing against each other. I closed my eyes.

But then I was kneeling somehow. Kneeling as if I'd been pushed to the ground. *Clattering, clattering, clattering.* Kneeling by the bin. Ketchupy chips strewn around me. My knees were wet. I was in the mud. Plastic pint cups. Cans. There was a seagull near. Too near. Pecking at the rubbish. I was clambering back, away from his beak, his cold prehistoric eyes.

Now Tom had *her* pressed against the bin. She had her head tipped back. She was in the blue hoodie she used to wear when she was eighteen. She is thin, her hair tousled, dreaded. Tom is kissing her, his hand down the front of *her* jeans. I'm shouting his name, but he can't hear me. Then, of course, just like she would in a dream, Sinead turns and looks at me.

I need to get in. Get into the cold water and make sense of things. I walk to edge of the the loch, wrap my clothes and both boots up in my jumper, and put it beside a rock. Then I make my way to where the bank slopes down into the water. I step one foot in. Freezing freezing freezing. Hurting my toes, my ankles. I put the other foot in and walk. By the time the water gets to my thighs, my toes have gone numb and are no longer screaming, but the tops of my legs are. I move faster, wading and stumbling. The freeze over my pelvis and stomach. Gasping. High-pitched cries into the still air. In in in. I plunge my chest under. Nothing but the cold. My shoulders are in and then all of me. The stillness as the cold coats the back of my head. Factory reset. Nothing but that coldness moving through my brain.

I resurface and hear myself shout out again. I rub my eyes, but I can no longer see the edge or my pile of clothes on the bank. The mist seems to have lowered, thickened, and there is just white. And then a bleating noise. The goat? But it's too close. Can goats swim? The bleat again. But it doesn't quite sound like a goat. It's too girlish, less like a bleat and more like a giggle. Another bleat to my right and a shifting in the mist. A shape coming through the water towards me. A head. Arms. And that bleating sound again.
Breyheheyeyeheh.
Her hair is wet and plastered to her scalp and face.

171

Brahhhahhhahhhahhh.

Sinead moves forwards and all at once she is beside me, her legs touching mine under the water. Then I am bleating too.

Bbbbrrreehehehe.

Rattling giggles and her face so close to mine. Now we are bleating together and I can feel my shoulders sinking lower and lower into the water. Our wet hair is mixing as wrists knock wrists, knock ribs, knock elbows. My fingers are in my mouth, then her mouth. And we are nuzzling, blurring into the slip and slide of wet bodies, sliding down and down and under –

Sinead's wet face. Then Tom's, with screws in his mouth, kneeling beside the broken wardrobe. What about a richness of martens? Is that a real one? Wren's voice, muffled and shouting: But I *need* the purple one. Alice murmuring and rearranging things as I tell her how good she is at believing in the future. Sinead's face again: I said repairing things, not – Wren: The *purple* one; Alice: Okay then, you have the purple one and I'll have the red. A darkening. A window. Screws in *my* mouth now as I look at my reflection and say it again: you are so good at believing in the –

I push up and out. Up and out and air. Gasping, panting, breathing. I spin around. Silence. The mist has lifted and I can see the bank again, and not even four feet away, the rock and my bundle of clothes.

I clamber out, freezing, and dry myself with my T-shirt. I shiver as I put on my pants, jeans, vest and jumper, then I sit and dry my feet. One sock, two socks. List five things that are true. One foot in one boot. One foot in the other boot. List them.

The water was cold. That's one. Two: I need to go inside somewhere and get warm. I rub the tops of my arms and pull my knees in to my chest. Three: I have matches and I know how to build a fire. The sea and the sound of the waves. Four: There will be a ferry in the morning. I will see it crossing the water. I begin to lace up my boots. Five. Five: If it's all true, all of it, even the bits that can't be – and not just for me, but for everybody – if all the opposites and the awfulness and the – if it's all true, and it's all true at the same time – if there's no such thing as properly, then there's just –

I stand up. I can work on number five once I've made the fire.

editions

Founded in 2007, CB editions publishes chiefly short
fiction and poetry, including work in translation.
Books can be ordered from www.cbeditions.com.